www.melvinbeederman.com

MELVIN BEEDERMAN
SUPERHERO

ATTACK OF THE VALLEY GIRLS

GREG TRINE

ILLUSTRATED BY
RHODE MONTIJO

SQUARE
FISH

HENRY HOLT AND COMPANY ★ NEW YORK

To my sister Teri
—G. T.

For my superfriends: Poochie,
Thunder Nerd, and Spork
—R. M.

SQUARE
FISH

An Imprint of Macmillan
175 Fifth Avenue, New York, NY 10010
mackids.com

Library of Congress Cataloging-in-Publication Data
Trine, Greg.
Attack of the Valley Girls / text by Greg Trine ; art by Rhode Montijo.
p.   cm.–(Melvin Beederman, superhero)
Summary: Valley Girls Chantelle and Brittany, under the influence of a mad
scientist's evil potion, hatch a plan to take over the city by kidnapping the
mayor's wiener dog, Schnitzel, but Melvin and his partner in uncrime,
Candace are on their trail.
ISBN 978-0-8050-8161-9
[1. Heroes–Fiction. 2. Dogs–Fiction. 3. Scientists–Fiction. 4. Los Angeles
(Calif.)–Fiction. 5. Humorous stories.]   I. Montijo, Rhode, ill. II. Title.
PZ7.T7356Att 2008   [Fic[–dc22   2007027315

Originally published in the United States by Henry Holt and Company
First Square Fish Edition: 2013
Hand-lettering by David Gatti
Square Fish logo designed by Filomena Tuosto

7   9   10   8

AR: 3.9 / LEXILE: 600L

CONTENTS

FIRST LAIR ON THE LEFT

"Up, up, and away."

Crash!

"Up, up, and away."

Splat!

"Up, up, and away."

Thud!

"Up, up, and away."

Kabonk!

This was how superhero Melvin Beederman always started his day—by trying to get off the ground and not doing a very good job of it. Actually, he started his day like everyone else in the world did—by waking up. Then he had a pretzel or two with his pet rat Hugo while watching a rerun of their favorite TV show, *The Adventures of Thunderman*.

But when he went to work it was fall-on-his-face time. It was crash-splat-thud-kabonk time.

Pretty embarrassing for a graduate of the Superhero Academy!

Melvin was up and flying on the fifth try and waved good-bye to Hugo. "Hold down the fort, big guy. I'm off to save the world."

"Squeak," replied the rat. This either

meant "As long as I have pretzels I'll do anything you say." Or maybe it was "Don't take any wooden Fig Newtons."

Melvin was never really sure what Hugo was saying. He was just glad to have somebody to watch cartoons with.

"Leave some pretzels for me," Melvin said as he zoomed away from his tree house hideout toward downtown Los Angeles. He was the superhero in charge of the city, along with his partner in uncrime, Candace Brinkwater.

Candace was not a graduate of the Superhero Academy. She lived in a normal house with a normal family and went to a normal school. But she was *anything* but normal. After all, she had once scored 500 points in a single game of basketball. She could run the hundred-yard dash in three and a half seconds. She was the only third-grader who could fly.

Melvin and Candace combined forces every day after she got out of school. Until then he was on his own.

Melvin flew over the city. It was a fine day for flying and a fine day for catching bad guys. It was *not* a fine day for seeing everyone's underwear. But that is what Melvin saw. He couldn't turn off his x-ray vision, so as he zoomed across the city and looked down he saw underwear—all sizes, all colors. And not all of it was clean. Some even had holes!

"Holy underwear!" Melvin said, trying to look away. "That's disgusting."

Holy underwear, indeed! It *was* disgusting. Even to the narrator.

"Now to catch a few bad guys," Melvin said to himself. Catching bad guys always made him feel better. He could almost forget about his x-ray vision problems. Almost.

But there were no bad guys to be found. No crimes were being committed. No bank robberies. No car thefts. Everyone seemed to be behaving. And as Melvin raced between the tall buildings of downtown, he thought only one thing— *Bo-ring!* How could he save the world if there was nothing to save it *from*?

Melvin saw a man walking his dog and dropped from the sky to ask him a question. "Sir, do you know of any criminals who need catching?"

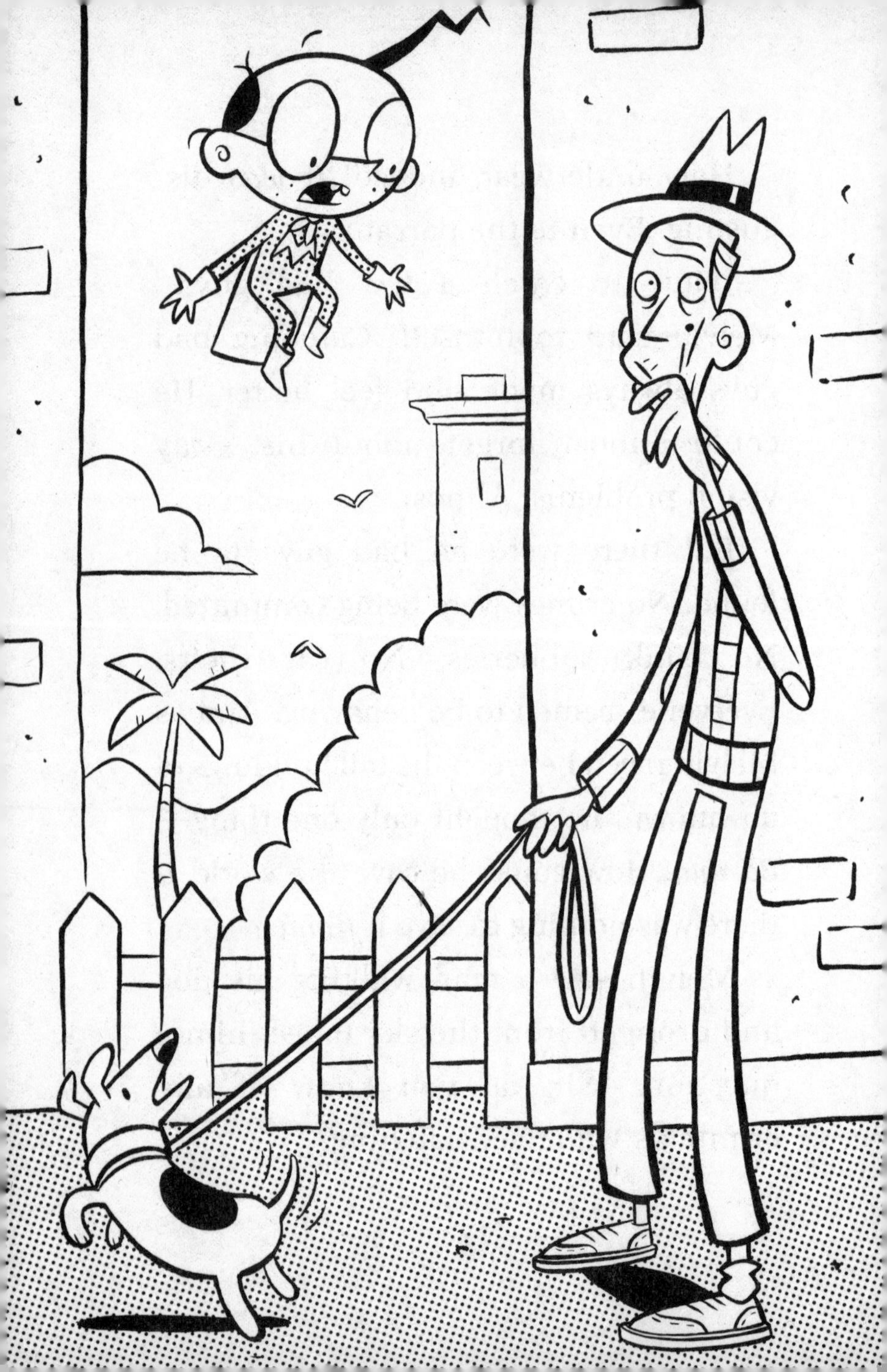

"Criminals?" the man asked.

"Yes, you know, bad guys—bank robbers, car thieves, drug dealers, folks who use bad language."

The man scratched his chin and thought. "My neighbor is a mad scientist. Does that count?"

Here was the break Melvin needed. Maybe this was someone planning on taking over the world, and Melvin would have to stop him! "Where does this mad scientist live?"

"Up the hill." The man pointed. "First lair on the left."

"Thanks." Melvin took off running. He decided to stay on the ground. He hated trying to launch himself in public.

THE MAD SCIENTIST'S SON

It was a big lair, as lairs go. "This mad scientist must be pretty successful," Melvin said to himself. And successful mad scientists were smart mad scientists. There might be booby traps designed to catch unsuspecting superheroes. Melvin had to be careful.

He crept up to the entrance of the lair. So far, so good. Melvin knocked on the door.

A young man opened it. He didn't look like a mad scientist at all. His hair was combed. His shirt was tucked in. He didn't wear glasses. The question was, Did he have an evil laugh? You could fake clothing and hygiene. But an evil laugh was a dead giveaway.

Melvin had to find out. "Hi. I'm from Jokemasters. What's black and white and red all over?"

"A newspaper?" the young man said.

"No, a zebra with a sunburn."

The young man laughed in a non-evil way. He didn't seem *MAD* at all. *Bo-ring.*

"Are you sure you're really from Jokemasters?" the young man asked. "You look a lot like Melvin Beederman, the superhero."

"Yes, I am Melvin Beederman," Melvin said. "I was just testing your sense of humor."

"Did I pass? After all, that was a pretty rotten joke."

"You passed."

"I'm Mike, Mr. Beederman. Would you like some tea? I have some brewing on the stove."

Melvin would have been way more interested if *trouble* had been brewing. But since there was no trouble to be found, tea would have to do.

Actually, trouble was always brewing . . . that's just how the world worked. The question was, Was it *brewed* yet? If it was brewed, then you had to watch out. If it was just brewing, you had time to prepare. One of the things that was brewing was that evil aliens were on their way to Earth. But they were very far away and hadn't kicked into Gamma Drive yet. Most likely, they wouldn't arrive until book seven or eight. And if they took a wrong turn at Alphacentory, they wouldn't make it at all!

But back to Melvin Beederman.

"Thanks," he said. "Tea would be great."

And so Melvin Beederman had tea with Mike, who didn't seem like a mad scientist at all. In fact, he was a pretty nice guy. If he had a cape, he'd make a great partner in uncrime, Melvin thought.

"Well, I'm off to save the world,"
Melvin said after a third cup of tea. He
went outside and waited for the young
man to close the door before trying to
launch himself.

"Up, up, and away."

Crash!

Three more tries.

Splat!
Thud!
Kabonk!

Melvin was up and flying on the fifth try. Hopefully there was a bad guy nearby who needed catching. More important, hopefully there was a *bathroom* nearby!

While Melvin was busy looking for bad guys . . . uh . . . a bathroom, things were really brewing at the mad scientist's lair he'd just left. And not just tea.

After the young man closed the front door, someone yelled, "Who was at the door, Mike?" It was his father, the real mad scientist in the family.

"Melvin Beederman. I invited him in for tea."

"You what?" His father couldn't believe his ears. And ears never lie! "He's a superhero! What kind of mad scientist are you?"

"I'm not a mad scientist," Mike said. "I'm just related to one."

This was their problem, of course. Mad scientist father had raised his son to follow in his evil footsteps, but the training didn't work. The son was about as evil as, well, Melvin Beederman.

"Something has to be done," the mad scientist father said to himself. He went into his evil laboratory and slammed the door. He began pouring things into a blender. He'd make his son more evil, one way or another.

"I'll make my son more evil—"

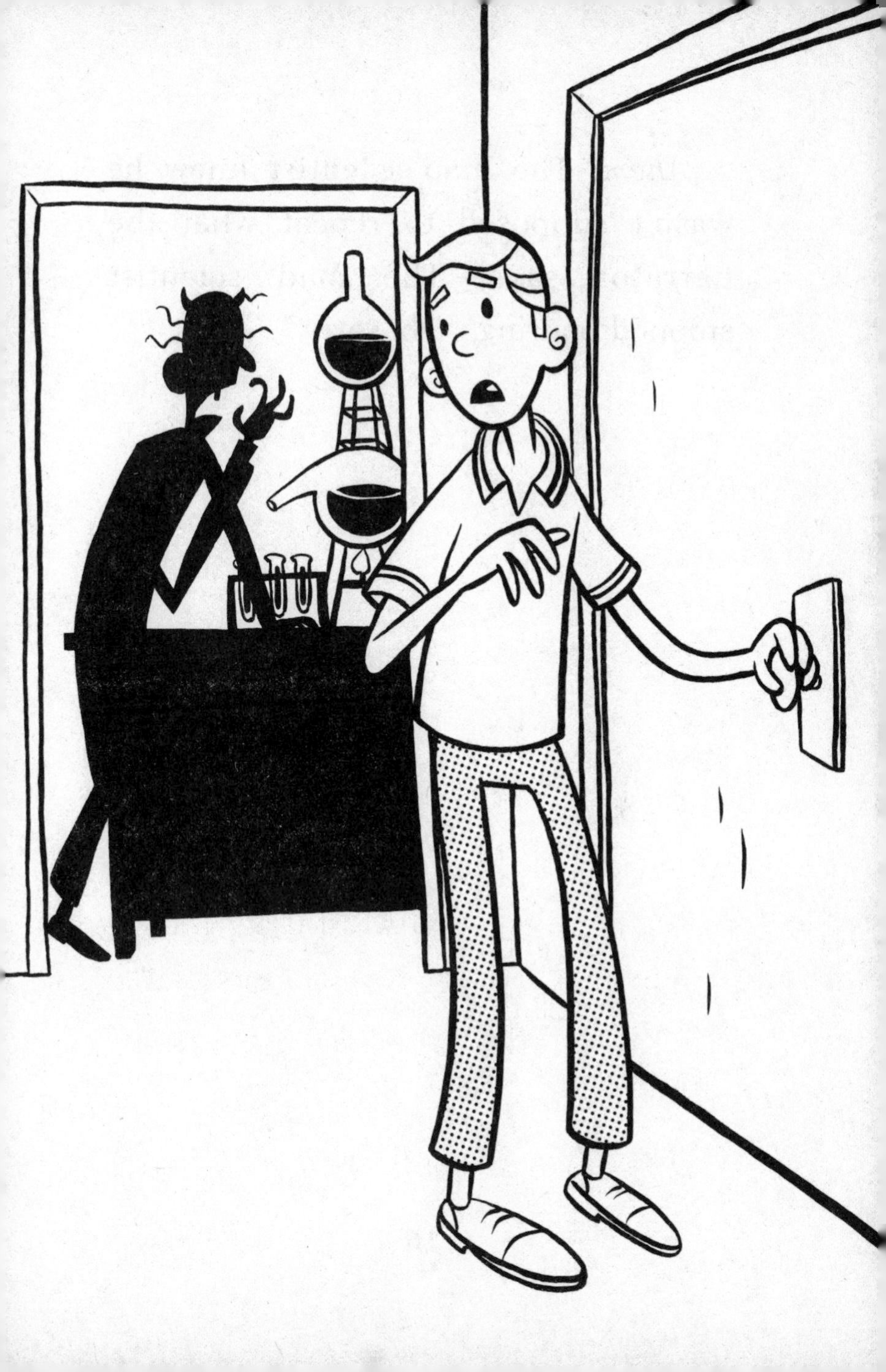

Ahem! The mad scientist knew he wasn't supposed to repeat what the narrator says. The mad scientist stopped pouring. "Oh, sorry."

THE MAD SCIENTIST'S EVIL POTION

Is it possible to make my son more evil with a special potion? thought the mad scientist. He worked all night, testing and retesting his mixtures. He was alone, except for his dog Schnitzel, who had come into the laboratory through the doggy door, looking for a snack. This is the number one rule of the Dog's Code: Beg for Food at all Times. The second rule is Steal Food if Begging Doesn't Work.

Schnitzel, who was a wiener dog, was using all his best moves—the sad puppy eyes, the whimper, the suck-it-in-and-look-skinny look—but nothing was working. The mad scientist was too busy concocting a make-my-son-more-evil potion to pay attention to his dog.

It was this same potion that Schnitzel was now eyeing. It looked like a milk shake. Something he'd enjoy. And after all, begging wasn't working. Didn't rule number two tell him what to do? As soon as the mad scientist turned his back, the dog jumped onto the workbench, grabbed the cup holding the milk shake . . . uh . . . potion, and ran out of the laboratory.

The mad scientist whirled around. "Come back here, you evil mutt!"

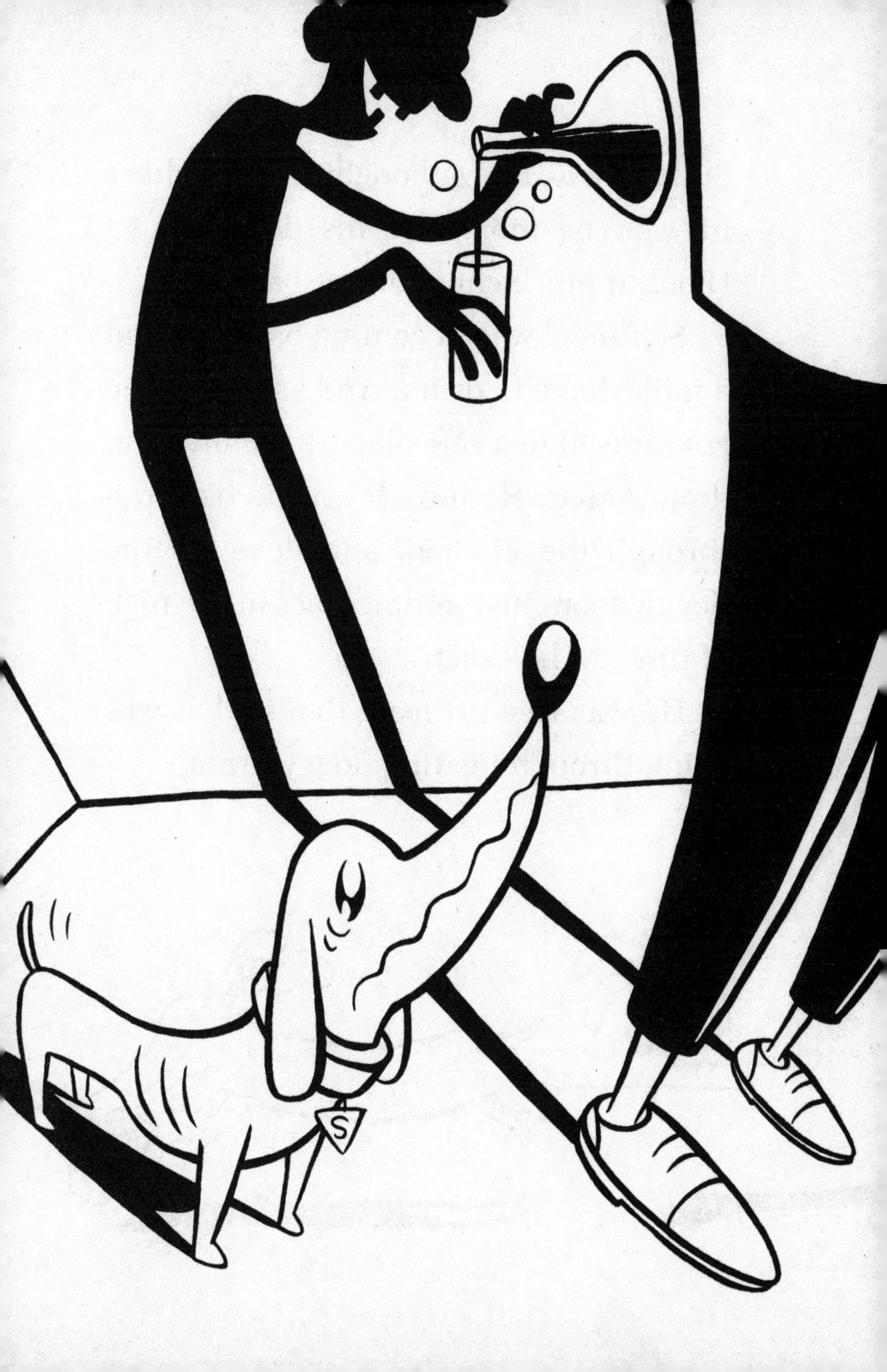
S

Suddenly, he had a thought. Why couldn't his son be more like his dog? But he shook it off. "Schnitzel, get back here."

Schnitzel wasn't coming back. He had a milk shake to drink. And as soon as he got himself to a safe place, he planned to do just that. He tore down the hall, ran through the kitchen, and dove for the doggy door. Just in time. Just in the nick of time, to be exact.

He was free. At least that's what was going through his tiny doggy brain.

Little did he know that high above him a hawk was circling and his tiny hawk brain was saying something like LOOK AT THE SIZE OF THAT RAT! Wiener dog, rat—this hawk didn't know the difference.

"Holy lunchtime," said the hawk. Actually, he said, "Caw!" or whatever sound hawks make. But he meant holy lunchtime. He swooped from the sky.

Holy lunchtime, indeed! Schnitzel never saw it coming. He was too busy thinking of the milk shake. That is, until he felt the hawk's talons sink into his fur. Before he could say "Excuse me, big guy, but would you mind removing your claws from my flesh?" he was flying high over Los Angeles and headed toward the Valley.

The hawk was soon joined by his best friend, who asked, "What's with the wiener dog?" Actually, what he said was "Caw!" But he meant what's with the wiener dog?

"Wiener dog? I thought it was a rat."

The second hawk shook his head. "Nope. Wiener dog."

That's when the hawk holding Schnitzel let go. And that's when Schnitzel let the milk shake go. And that's when the cup holding the potion landed in the chicken feed of Fester's Fine Chicken Farm and Tractor Repair. Luckily, Schnitzel landed in a nearby tree, which broke his fall. But the chicken feed was now contaminated with the mad scientist's evil potion. This contaminated the chickens, who started swearing a lot and picking fights. Some of them wanted to start wearing leather jackets and riding motorcycles.

Worst of all, the potion contaminated the eggs that the chickens laid. And these eggs were used to make chocolate chip cookies. Cookies eaten by local teenagers. Don't ask how, but it went very fast, from potion to eggs to cookies to teenagers.

Two Valley girls in particular. Their names were Chantelle and Brittany, and they were sitting in the cafeteria of East Valley High School. Not only were they friends, but they also lived in the same foster home, since both of them did not have parents.

"Hey, like, do you want half of this cookie?" Chantelle asked her friend.

"Like, totally," Brittany replied.

This was part of the Valley Girl's Code—say "like" and "totally" a lot. There were other parts to the code, such as Hang Out at the Mall a Lot and Flick Your Hair as Often as Possible, but we'll get to that later.

The two girls bit into the cookie made with the eggs contaminated by the mad scientist's evil potion. The change was immediate. Their eyes clouded over. Devious and sinister thoughts hit them all at once.

"How about we, like, take over the city?" Brittany said.

"That would be, like, totally cool!"

After school they headed to the mall to make plans. Neither of them had ever taken over a whole city before. This was exciting stuff!

SINISTER SISTERS

While Chantelle and Brittany were plotting to take over Los Angeles, Melvin Beederman was meeting with his partner in uncrime Candace Brinkwater. They met in the library every day after school so that Melvin could help her with math. This was their agreement. After doing her math homework, the two of them would set off to save the world.

"How did it go today, Melvin?" Candace asked.

"Not much happening. I didn't see one bad guy all day." Melvin was feeling kind of low. Catching bad guys was what he did best. What did you do when there weren't any to catch?

"What about those evil aliens coming to take over the planet?"

"What evil aliens?" Melvin asked. The librarian walked by, and he tried not to look at her underwear, which wasn't easy. "Candace, have you been talking to the narrator again?"

"Oops."

When they finished math, they went outside and launched themselves. At least, Candace did.

"Up, up, and away."

Crash!

"Up, up, and away."

Splat!

On the fifth try Melvin was up and flying. "Now to find some bad guys," he said. "I wish those aliens would get here already." Melvin had never battled aliens before. Neither had Candace. But they were always open to new experiences. "I just wish trouble was brewing someplace besides outer space. I don't want to have to wait until book seven or eight to catch a bad guy."

⋀⋀

Trouble *was* brewing, of course. It was brewing just north of Los Angeles, in the Valley. Chantelle and Brittany were at the mall, planning on taking over the city. But first things first. They needed a lair.

"I know, like, the perfect place for our lair," Brittany said.

"Where?" asked Chantelle.

"How about, like, the girl's dressing room at Macy's?"

"Perfect. You grab some jeans and I'll grab some sweaters and I'll meet you there." As long as they were going to make their lair inside a dressing room, they might as well try on clothes.

They found an empty dressing room and went in, closing the door behind them.

"Okay," Chantelle said, "like, what's the plan?"

Brittany was looking at herself in the mirror, checking out the sweater she'd just put on.

"Would you, like, pay attention, Brittany? If we're going to take over the city, we need a plan."

Brittany flicked her hair. "Hmmm. . . . there's only one thing to do."

"What?" Chantelle had put on some jeans and was now turning from side to side. "Is my butt too big?"

Totally, Brittany thought, but she didn't say it. "We wait until dark, then go to the narrator's house and sneak a

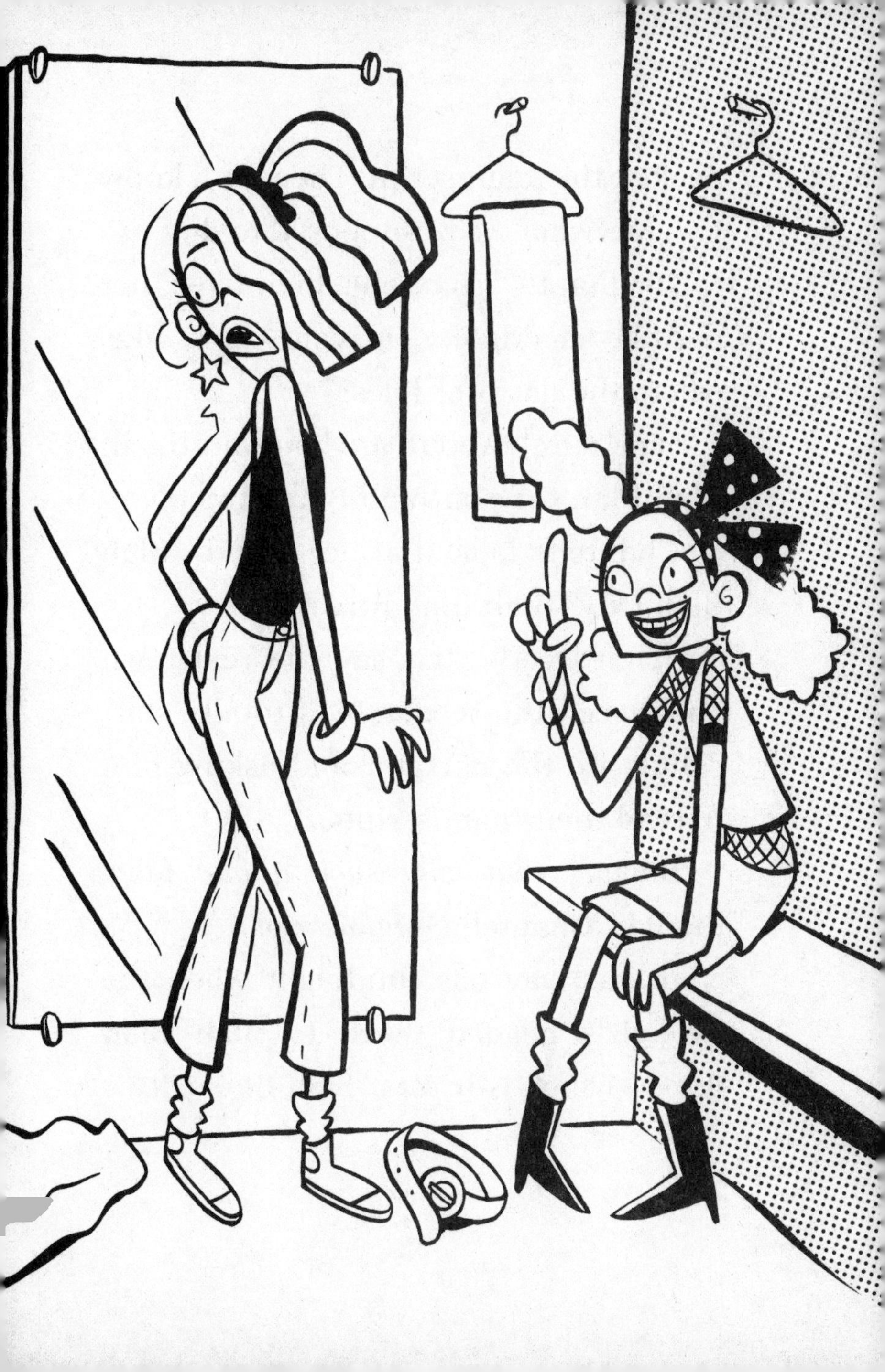

peek at the manuscript. Then we'll know for sure what we're supposed to do."

"Brilliant!" Chantelle high-fived her partner in crime. "Do you know, like, where the narrator lives?"

"For sure! About an hour north, in Blah Blah City, on Blah Blah Street."

Chantelle looked at her friend. "Blah Blah City? Blah Blah Street?"

"That's code. If I say the real town and street, the readers will totally start calling up the narrator and asking him to read their manuscripts."

Hmmm, that isn't such a bad idea, thought Chantelle. *Manuscripts.*

It was way past midnight when the two girls headed north to Blah Blah Street, which is in East Blah Blah City.

MEANWHILE . . .

While Chantelle and Brittany were headed north to Blah Blah, Schnitzel the dog was still trying to get down from the tree he'd fallen into when the hawk let go of him. It wasn't easy. He'd been stuck in the tree for days. Finally, he decided to jump and take his chances.

He landed with a thud—a very loud thud. A thud so loud that two owls, who were perched on top of Farmer Fester's barn, looked over.

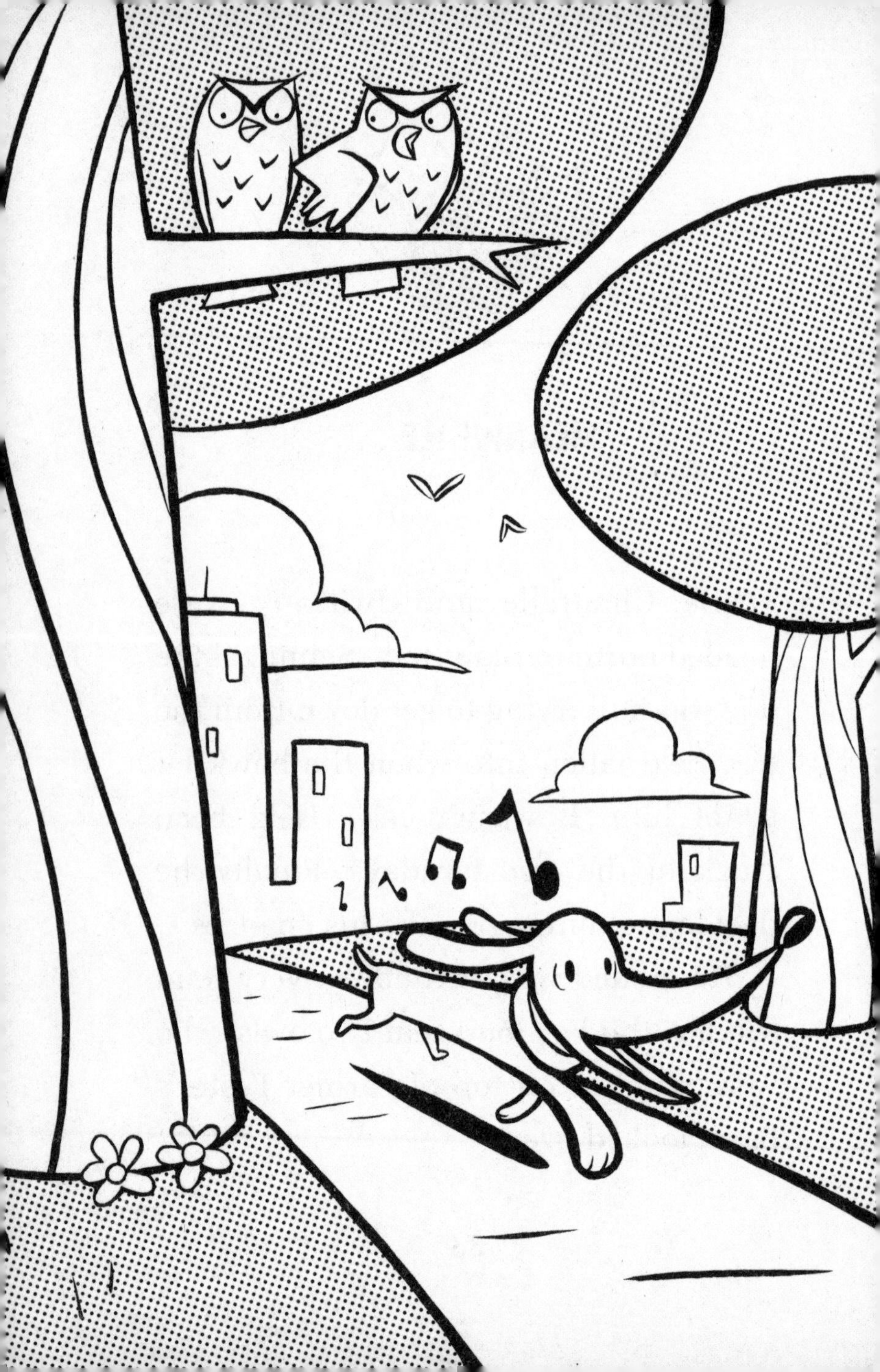

One owl nudged his buddy. "Hey, is that a rat?"

"No, it's a wiener dog."

Actually what they said was "hoo-hoo" and "hoo-hoo," but it meant "Hey, is that a rat? No, it's a wiener dog."

After all he'd been through, Schnitzel was now very cautious. He'd already been plucked by a hawk, and he wasn't going to let that happen again. He walked along singing "I Am a Wiener Dog, Not a Rat" just in case any birds of prey had different thoughts on the subject.

The question was how to make it back to the mad scientist's lair. He hadn't been paying attention when the hawk had snatched him. Where was he, exactly? Fester's Fine Chicken Farm and Tractor

Repair, but where was that? And which way should he go?

He decided to guess, and hope he got lucky. If all went well, he'd be home before sunrise.

"Are you sure he's a wiener dog?" said one of the owls, watching Schnitzel leave.

"Trust me," said the other owl.

Brittany and Chantelle pulled up in front of the narrator's house on Blah Blah Street, on the east side of Blah Blah. The house was completely dark.

"Are you, like, totally sure about this?" whispered Chantelle. "I've never, like, broken into a house before."

"Yes, I'm sure. We won't know how to

take over the city if we don't take a look
at the manuscript."

The two girls crept around to the side
of the house, looking for an unlocked
window. They found one and slid it open.

Chantelle climbed in first. Brittany used the tiny light on her key chain to show the way.

Loud snoring was coming from one of the bedrooms. Brittany nodded toward it. "Narrator," she whispered.

They found what looked like an office on the other side of the house and began snooping around.

Brittany shone the tiny light on the desk. And there it was—the manuscript. "Got it."

Brittany began turning pages. Midway through the story they learned what they had to do in order to take over Los Angeles. "Okay, let's go. We found what we were looking for."

"Hold on. Let's take a peek at the ending."

Brittany shook her head. "Uh-uh, that would be cheating."

"We're *already* cheating!"

"Good point." Brittany came closer, but stopped herself. "No, we can't. I want a little mystery in this thing."

So does the reader.

The girls turned to leave. Then Chantelle saw something. "Hey!" she whispered. She pointed to another manuscript. "It's book eight."

"So?"

"So let's take a look. I want to see if the aliens make it to Earth. What if they take a wrong turn at Alphacentory?"

Brittany grabbed Chantelle. "We don't have time. The narrator might wake up."

Chantelle nodded. "Okay, but I have to go to the bathroom first."

"Meet you at the car." Brittany left the office in a hurry.

Chantelle flipped through the pages of book eight. It was going to be the best one yet! Then another piece of paper caught her eye. It described something called Gamma Drive—how it worked and how to install it. This could come in handy in auto shop, she thought. She grabbed the instructions and stuffed them into her pocket.

But before she joined Brittany outside, she had one more thing to do. She pulled a short story she'd been working on out of her purse and left it on the narrator's desk. Then she scribbled a little note.

Dear Narrator,

Please read my

story and tell me

what you think

of it.

Yours truly,

Chantelle

BAD-GUY–CATCHING BLUES

What to do when you're fresh out of bad guys? This was Melvin Beederman's problem. He paced back and forth in his tree house. "What do you think I should do, Hugo?" he asked his rat.

"Squeak," said Hugo. Most likely this meant "Don't bother me while *The Adventures of Thunderman* is on." Though it might have meant "What are you going to be for Halloween?"

Melvin decided maybe watching TV

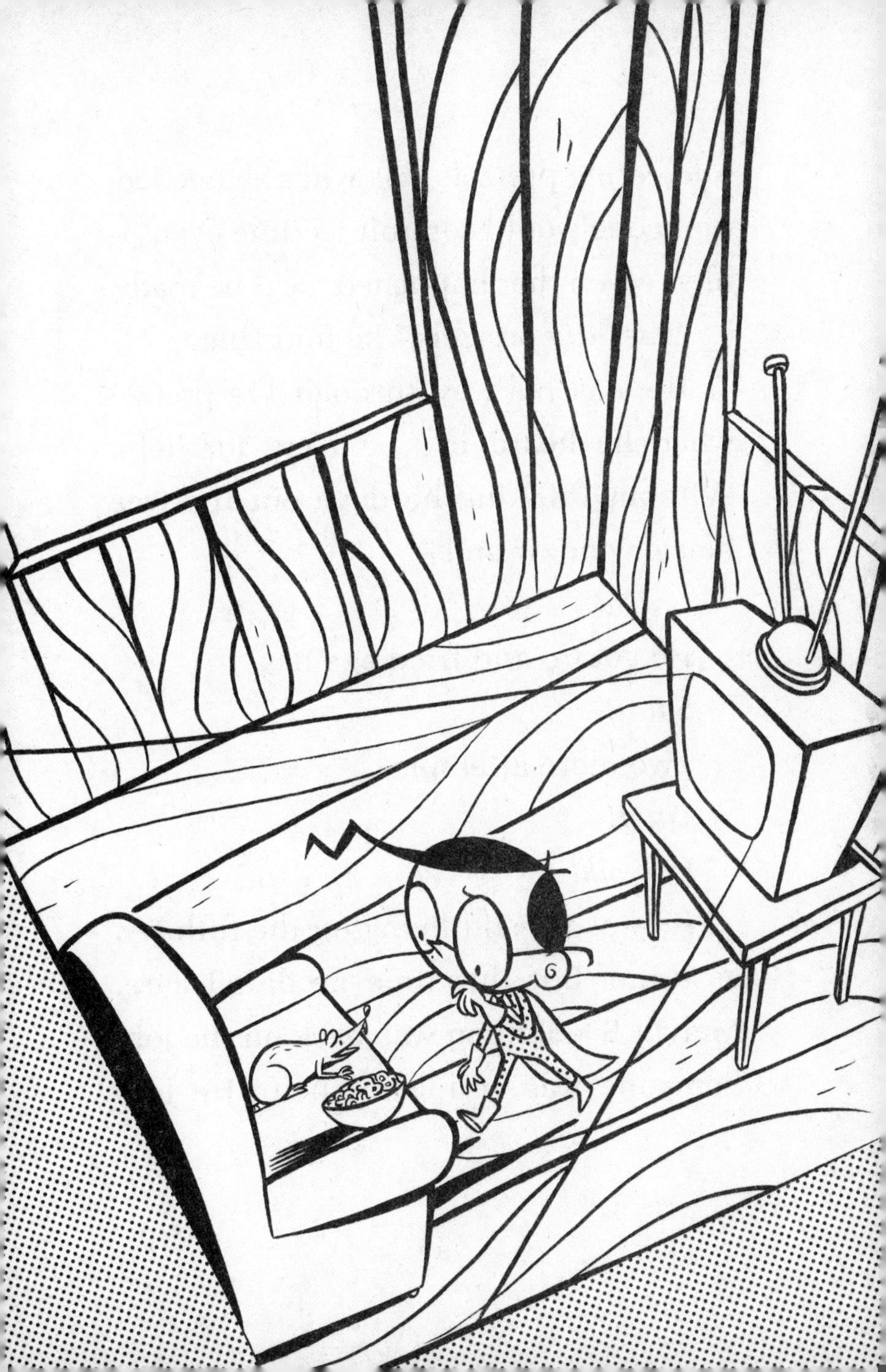

and eating pretzels was what he needed. Someone would commit a crime eventually. When that happened, he'd be ready.

"Pass the pretzels," he told Hugo.

He was halfway through his pretzel when he heard it . . . a cry for help. Without thinking he dove out the tree house window and—

Crash!

He got up and tried again.

Splat!

Two more attempts.

Thud!

Kabonk!

He was up and flying on the fifth try, as usual. But this time he didn't care. Melvin Beederman was back on the job. Someone was crying for help. He just hoped whatever it was had on clean underwear.

⋀⋀

Melvin was back doing what he did best, but all was not well for Schnitzel the wiener dog. Not only did he spend the night singing "I Am a Wiener Dog, Not a Rat," but no less than eleven times he stopped to howl at the moon, just to make the point that he wasn't a rodent.

The local birds of prey seemed to be getting the message that he was indeed a dog. For the local rat community it was a different story. Schnitzel fell in with a group of Alley Rats who tried to recruit him as their new leader.

"Listen," the leader rat had said,

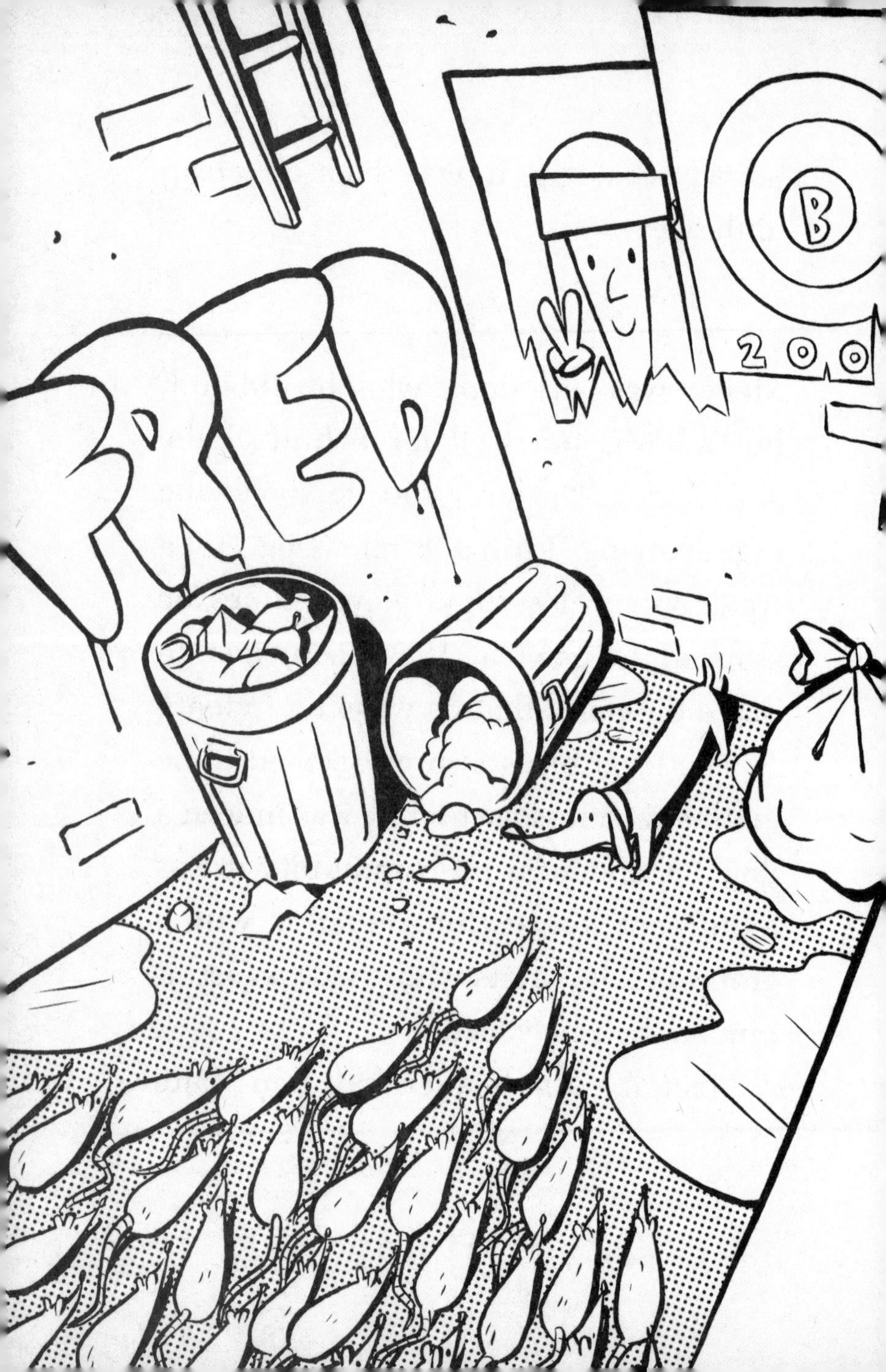
FRED
B
200

"you're the biggest rat any of us have ever seen. You can help us in our revolt against the Alley Cats."

"I AM NOT A RAT!" Schnitzel yelled, and he howled at the moon just to prove it.

The rats didn't believe him. They all howled at the moon to prove they could do just as good a job. They couldn't. It was only a bunch of squeaking, and it was very annoying to anyone who was not a rat.

But all this was not the worst of Schnitzel's misadventures. The worst part came later, when a rat named Geraldine developed a crush and began batting her eyelashes at him. Poor Schnitzel! The last thing he needed was a girlfriend—especially one who was a rat. He had to find the mad scientist's lair. And he had to find it quick.

"Taxi!" he yelled as a yellow car zoomed past. The taxi didn't stop. They never do for rats.

THE VALLEY GIRLS' SINISTER PLAN

Now that Chantelle and Brittany had seen the manuscript, they knew exactly what to do in order to take over the city.

"We know just what to do," said Chantelle. She didn't know that she wasn't supposed to repeat what the narrator says. She didn't even know that she wasn't supposed to sneak a peek at the manuscript! What if it was only a rough draft? What if their idea got edited out later? This was confusing stuff.

That afternoon Chantelle tossed a note onto Brittany's desk during Mr. Meckleroony's pottery-making class. It said, "When do we start Operation Take-Over-the-City?"

Brittany tossed another note back. "Devious and sinister plans are never discussed outside of the lair." This was a rule that she had just made up. The fact was she wanted to get to Macy's as soon as possible. There was a jeans sale going on and she had to get there before everything got picked over.

After school the two girls walked to the mall and entered their lair. Brittany started trying on jeans immediately.

"Now, according to the narrator's manuscript, we have to kidnap the mayor's dog and hold him for ransom until they give us control of the city," Chantelle said.

Brittany examined herself in the full-length mirror. She wondered if her butt looked big but she didn't say anything. She did not want a second opinion on *THAT* subject.

"Are you listening, Brittany?"

"Yes, we kidnap the dog. Got it. Do you know where the mayor lives? And don't tell me Blah Blah Street."

"I will by tonight," Chantelle said. They couldn't begin Operation Take-Over-the-City until after midnight. In the meantime there was only one thing to do: Shop!

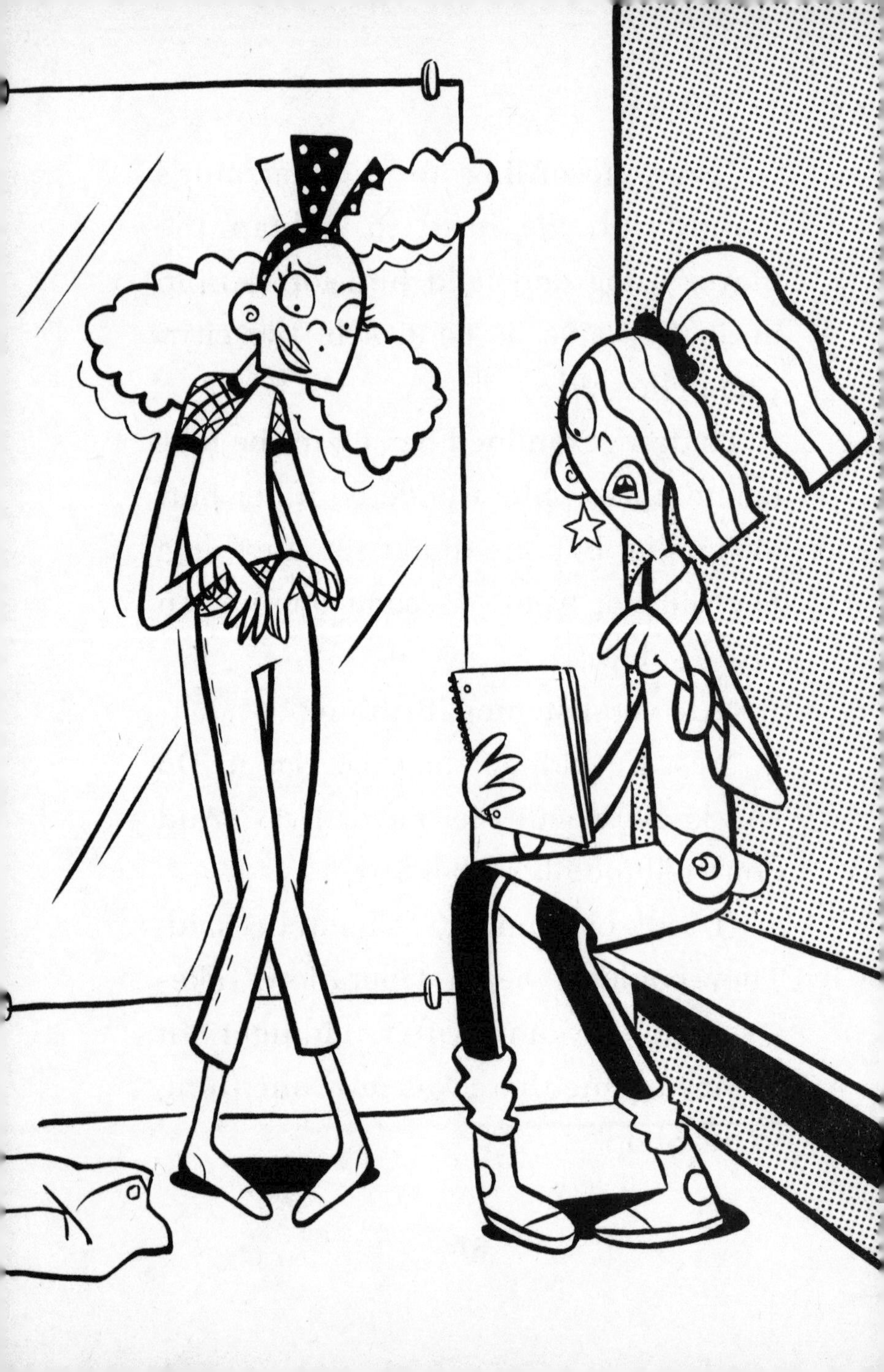

It was well past midnight when the two girls set off for the mayor's house. He didn't live on Blah Blah Street. He lived on Blankety Blank Street, just north of Blah Blah. This was in the Hollywood Hills.

Brittany drove while Chantelle scanned the houses for the address. The Hollywood Hills was where many movie stars lived. Chantelle was glad she was wearing her new jeans.

"I'm glad I'm wearing my new je—"

Ahem!

"Was that the narrator?" Brittany asked, keeping her eyes on the road.

"Yes. He hates when I repeat what he says."

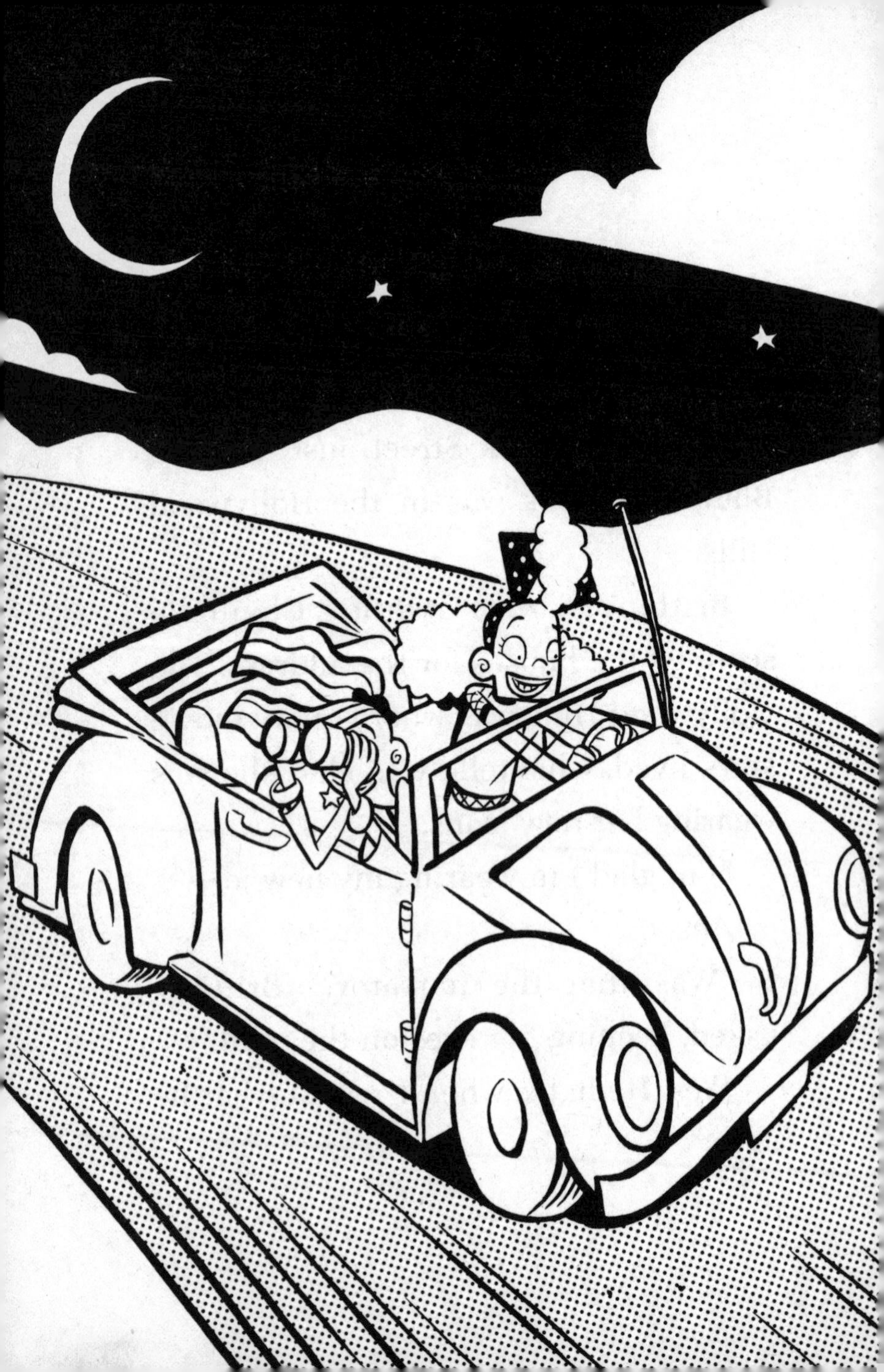

"I don't blame him. It is kind of annoying."

They drove on and on looking for the mayor's address on Blankety Blank Street, which, as everyone knows, is just north of Blah Blah.

"I am a wiener dog, not a rat." Schnitzel stopped singing, looked up at the moon, and howled. You never know when birds of prey are in the neighborhood, and Schnitzel wasn't taking any chances. So far his luck had held out. No hawks or owls were circling. And he had finally escaped from the rats who wanted him to lead them in their revolt against the Alley Cats.

He'd also given the slip to the rat who had a crush on him. He had no time for a girlfriend. Plus, she had the most annoying squeaky voice, not to mention she smelled like cheese!

But now Schnitzel was alone . . . in the middle of the night . . . in the middle of an unknown part of the city. If only he could find his way back. If only he could find something that looked familiar. If only he could—

Wait a minute! Schnitzel found himself gazing up at an enormous hill. He'd seen this place before. "Holy hilltop," he said. "I'm almost home."

Holy hilltop, indeed! This was one smart dog. *Ooo-oow!*

Oops. It was the dog that howled at the moon, not the narrator.

Schnitzel looked up at the moon and howled. *Ooo-oow.* He was almost home. He could hardly wait to see his mad scientist master again. He could hardly wait to get his paws on another milk shake.

TROUBLE AT BERT'S

While the two Valley girls were searching for the mayor's address, and while Schnitzel was making his way up an enormous hill, a rat and a superhero were snoring away in their tree house hideout. Actually, it was the rat who was doing the snoring. For a little guy, he sure could make a racket. This made it hard for Melvin Beederman to sleep. He got up and looked at his tired face in the mirror.

"Holy circles-under-my-eyes," he

said. "Hugo, will you knock off that snoring!"

Holy circles-under-his-eyes, indeed! Yeah, Hugo, pipe down.

Hugo didn't pipe down. And so Melvin turned on the TV and grabbed some leftovers from dinner. He had made Hugo's favorite, Pretzel à la King. It was cold now, but Melvin didn't care. He found a cartoon and settled in for a long sleepless night. But . . .

Something was wrong!

It wasn't the cold Pretzel à la King. It wasn't Hugo's snoring. Melvin couldn't put his finger on it, but something felt different. Trouble was brewing, of course. This was what Melvin was feeling. He leapt to his feet.

"Hot diggity! Trouble is brewing!"

Superheroes don't usually celebrate trouble, but it had been a while since he'd had a real mission, and he couldn't help himself. He began doing the dance of the unbored superhero. This shook the whole tree house and woke up the snoring Hugo.

"Squeak?" Hugo said, which either meant "Stop that racket; I'm trying to snore" or "Do you know how to tango?"

Melvin didn't know how to tango, but he did know the Superhero Shuffle. "Hugo, trouble is brewing. I've got work to do."

Melvin didn't know what the trouble was just yet. But he could feel his noggin power getting ready to kick in.

"My noggin power is about to kick in," he said.

The narrator didn't mind that Melvin repeated him this once. It was just that Melvin was sleepy and forgot the rules.

Melvin climbed down from the tree house and launched himself.

"Up, up, and away."

Crash!

Splat!

Thud!

Kabonk!

You might think that it would take him more than five tries to get up and flying since he was so tired. And this may be true, but the narrator couldn't think up any more cool sound effects to go with *crash, splat, thud,* and *kabonk,* so let's just leave it at that.

Melvin was up and flying on the . . . ahem . . . fifth try. He zoomed over the city looking for whatever trouble was brewing. This wasn't easy, since he hadn't exactly heard a cry for help. It was just a feeling that something wasn't quite right.

But what was it? And where?

He streaked across the sky, darting in and out between the tall buildings. The moon was shining and Melvin could see his reflection in the windows. He stopped to flex. Doing this was not part of the Superhero's Code. It was just a Melvin thing.

Suddenly he heard glass breaking and angry voices. It was coming from Bert's Bar and Grill, where their slogan was *Come to Bert's and Spend Money*. Melvin didn't have any money, but he knew the sound of a bar fight when he heard one.

He dropped from the sky just in time. Just in the nick of time to be exact. An angry man was holding a broken root beer bottle and threatening someone else with the jagged edges.

"Not so fast!" said Melvin, which was part of the Superhero's Code. You had to say this to give the bad guy a chance to do the right thing.

This bad guy didn't. He turned

toward Melvin and growled. He actually
growled! Like a lion. Like a tiger. Like a
bear. Oh my!

"Who said that?" the man with the
bottle asked.

"Who said what?" Melvin asked.

"Who said, 'Oh my'?"

"The narrator," Melvin said. "He gets carried away sometimes. Are you going to drop that bottle or not?"

"Not!"

"Thought so." And that's when Melvin Beederman delivered the famous Melvin Chop. Then he helped Bert put things back in order.

"How can I ever thank you?" Bert asked.

"Just doing my job, sir." This was also part of the Superhero's Code. Melvin always kept to the code.

The bar was put back in order, and the band began to play again. Melvin took out his harmonica and played with them. But something was still not right. The bar fight wasn't the trouble that he had felt was brewing. There was something else.

Melvin knew this the way he knew what it felt like to go *Splat*. He said good-bye to the band members after a few songs and went outside. Something bigger was coming.

And he had no idea what it was.

A GOOD NIGHT FOR A DOGNAPPING

"We're getting closer," Brittany said.

"How do you know?" Chantelle kept searching for the mayor's address.

"I can feel it. Valley girl's intuition."

Chantelle didn't know if there was such a thing. She was happy to be getting closer to taking over the city. She had never done this before and she just adored new experiences.

"Slow down," Chantelle said. "I think that's it up ahead."

Brittany stopped the car in front of the mayor's house. "I'm, like, excited. How about you?"

"Like, totally!"

The two girls made their way around the side of the house, checking for an open window. Every window in the place was locked. Fortunately, the back door was not.

"Holy easy-breaking-and-entering!" Chantelle said. "Our evil plan is working."

Holy easy-breaking-and-entering, indeed! Their evil plan *was* working. This was what you call beginner's luck.

Brittany opened the back door to the mayor's house and went inside, followed by Chantelle.

"Like, what's the plan?" Chantelle whispered.

"We kidnap the dog and make our demands to take over the city. Does that sound right to you?"

"Totally."

The two girls crept down the hall and into the living room. They found no sign of a dog, or any other kind of animal. Brittany suddenly stopped and looked at her friend. "What if his dog is a pit bull or a Rottweiler?"

"It means we better come up with a new plan."

"We can't. The narrator's manuscript said we kidnap the dog."

"Unless it was a first draft. Maybe he'll cut the dog thing later."

"This sure is complicated."

"You're telling me!"

They searched and searched in the dark house for the mayor's dog, hoping it was something other than a pit bull or Rottweiler.

As they say, being eaten alive can ruin your whole day.

⋀⋀

While Brittany and Chantelle were busy searching the mayor's house for a dog to kidnap, Schnitzel was making his way up a very familiar but very enormous hill. It was slow going, since he had to keep his eyes on the sky for birds of prey. He also made frequent stops to howl at the moon, sing his "I'm Not a Rat" song, and pee on every fire hydrant he saw. One way or another, he was getting the message across that he was, in fact, a dog.

It seemed to be working. The hawks and owls ignored him. So did the rats. After a while Schnitzel began recognizing trees and fire hydrants from when the mad scientist took him for walks after a long day of trying to take over the world. *Almost home*, he told himself. He quickened his pace, no longer howling, singing, or peeing. Okay, he did stop to pee once, but that's all. He was a dog on a mission.

Finally, he reached the long driveway of the mad scientist's house . . . uh . . . lair. He went around to the back and shoved himself through the doggy door into the kitchen.

Home at last! He bent down to kiss the floor. And that's when he heard the voices.

"It's the dog. Grab him, Chantelle! And gag him while you're at it."

"Gag him?"

"Yes, it's part of the Kidnapper's Code."

A pair of hands picked Schnitzel off the floor. Someone tied a handkerchief around his snout. He looked around the dark kitchen. Maybe he was in the wrong house. But, no, this *was* the right house— it had to be. His doggy dish was right there with his name on it—Schnitzel.

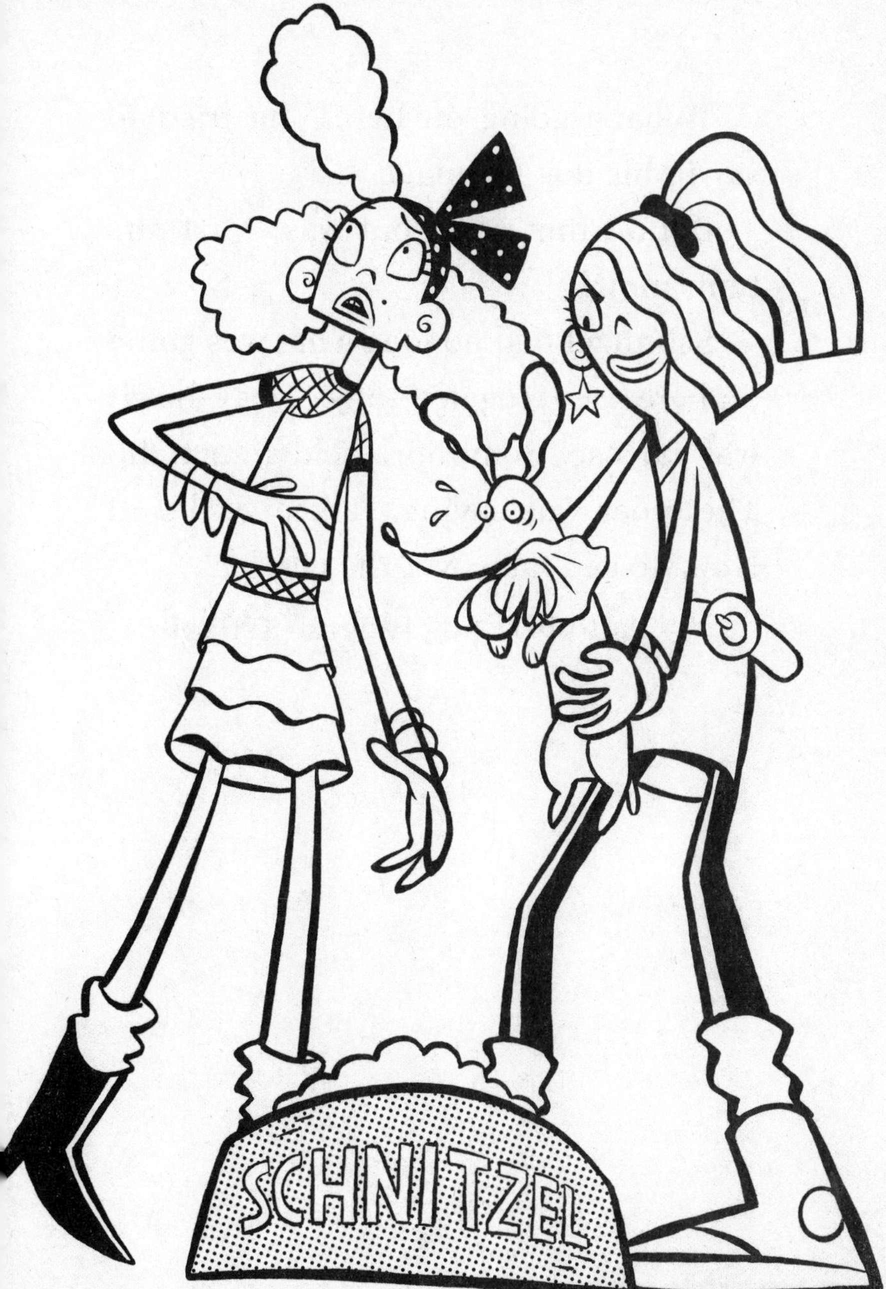
SCHNITZEL

"What's going on here?" he tried to say in his dog language.

But all that came out was "Mrrf mrr mmr mmrf."

Schnitzel had no idea what was going on here. He struggled to get away, but it was no use. Some girl held him tight. The other was saying, "Like, we did it! Now we can take over the city."

"Like, totally," the first girl replied.

ONE DAY ... OR ELSE!

Yes, the mayor of Los Angeles and the mad scientist were one and the same person. Being the mayor was just his day job. He was really a mad scientist at heart.

Word about Schnitzel spread quickly. The guy on the morning news show said, "Mayor's dog kidnapped. Details after this word from Bert's Bar and Grill."

The newspaper headlines read "Kidnappers Attempt Takeover by Stealing Mayor's Dog."

It wasn't long before the chief of police called Melvin Beederman. Melvin was having his breakfast and watching a rerun of *The Adventures of Thunderman* with Hugo when the phone rang.

"Melvin, we need your help," the chief of police said. "Someone has kidnapped the mayor's dog and is trying to take over the city."

"Ha! I *knew* trouble was brewing." Melvin tried not to sound excited. After all, poor Schnitzel could be in danger. But Melvin couldn't help himself. Finally, he had a real mission, something worthy of his superhero powers. "Don't worry, Your Highness, I'm on the job."

"Your Highness?"

"I mean, Your Chief-of-Policeness."

"That's better."

Melvin hung up the phone and turned to Hugo. "Gotta go catch a bad guy or two."

"Squeakity squeak squeak," Hugo said. This either meant "You just saved the world yesterday" or "I need a back rub."

Melvin didn't have time to figure out what his rat was trying to say. He had a city to save, and a wiener dog to rescue.

"Up, up, and away." He threw himself out of the tree house.

Like always, he was up and flying in five. He zoomed, he streaked, he zigged, he zagged. He had to find those kidnappers before they did something devious and sinister to the mayor's dog—or worse, before they took over the city.

The kidnappers had given the mayor one day to make up his mind, otherwise it would be curtains for his beloved Schnitzel.

"Holy I-only-have-one-day," said

Melvin, looking down at the people of Los Angeles and seeing way too much underwear. "That's not long."

Holy he-only-has-one-day, indeed! It *wasn't* long. Better get cracking, Melvin.

Melvin did. Or at least he tried to. He'd need his partner in uncrime to solve this one.

Now that Chantelle and Brittany had Schnitzel, they could no longer use the dressing room at Macy's as their lair. Instead, they used Chantelle's bedroom, which was right down the hall from Brittany's.

The two girls kept the dog gagged so that he wouldn't make any noise. They only took the handkerchief off to feed him. Everything was going as planned. In another day the city would be theirs.

Little did they know that Schnitzel was plotting his escape. That's not to say his escape attempt would be successful. He was just planning it.

They also didn't know that Melvin Beederman was on the job, and if anyone could stop them, he could—with the help of his partner in uncrime, Candace Brinkwater, of course.

Brittany turned to Chantelle. "What should we call ourselves?"

"What do you mean?"

"I mean when we take over the city. We can't call ourselves mayor. That's too boring."

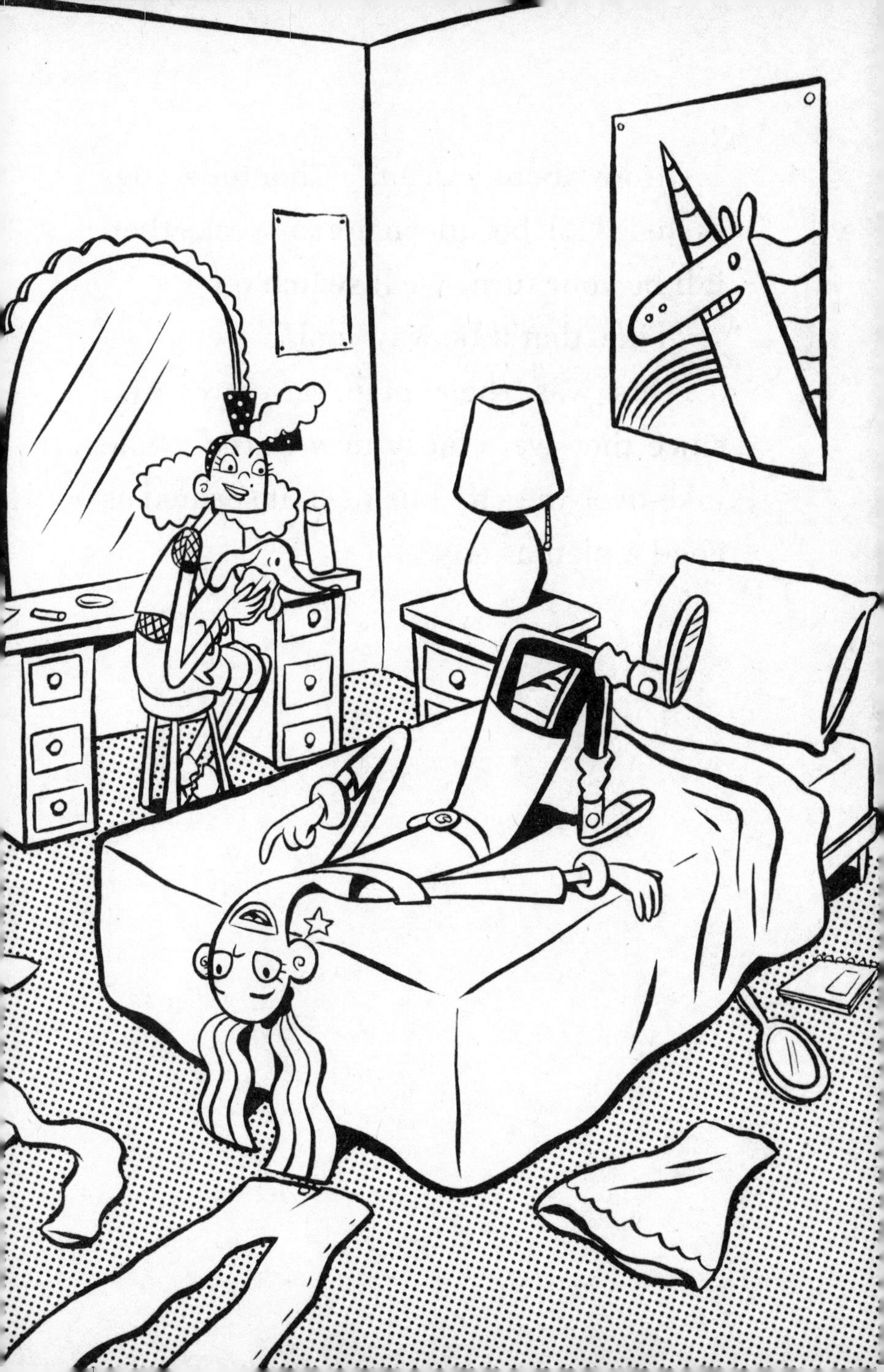

"How about queen?" Chantelle suggested. "I'll be queen for a week, then it'll be your turn. We'll switch off."

"Like, that'll be way cool."

This was their plan, anyway. And since they were fairly new to the whole take-over-the-city business, it seemed as good a plan as any.

DOCTOR DOOLITTLE, I PRESUME?

Tick tick tick. That's the clock ticking. The narrator is trying to make the reader anxious about the mayor's dog, Schnitzel.

Time was running out, and Melvin Beederman hadn't turned up anything. He'd spent the morning talking to people in the mayor's neighborhood. Maybe someone had seen something—a mysterious car, a stranger in a trench coat with dark glasses and a fake mustache.

Pick a cliché, any cliché.

No one had seen a thing. *The kidnappers must be pros*, Melvin thought. Which meant that if they didn't get what they wanted, they'd do what they said they'd do. They'd kill Schnitzel. Or worse—they'd make him do homework!

At three o'clock he met Candace Brinkwater at the local library. He filled her in on the case.

"You know what I think?" she said.

"What?"

"If this dog is in danger, maybe we should skip math today."

"What about your math grade?"

"What if they kill the dog? Or worse—what if they feed him junk food?"

"Hey, don't knock it. I eat pretzels all day long."

Candace thought this over. "Hmm . . . good point." She was rather fond of pretzels herself.

They skipped math anyway. The case was too important. So was Schnitzel.

Their plan was to continue doing what Melvin had started—interviewing people in the mayor's neighborhood. So far, no one had seen anything, but the superheroes had to keep looking.

Tick tick tick. Are you getting anxious? Good.

Time was indeed running out. Melvin and Candace decided to split up. "You take Maple Street," Melvin said. "And I'll take Mills and Telegraph."

All afternoon they interviewed people. Fat people, skinny people, people who climbed on rocks. But no one had seen a

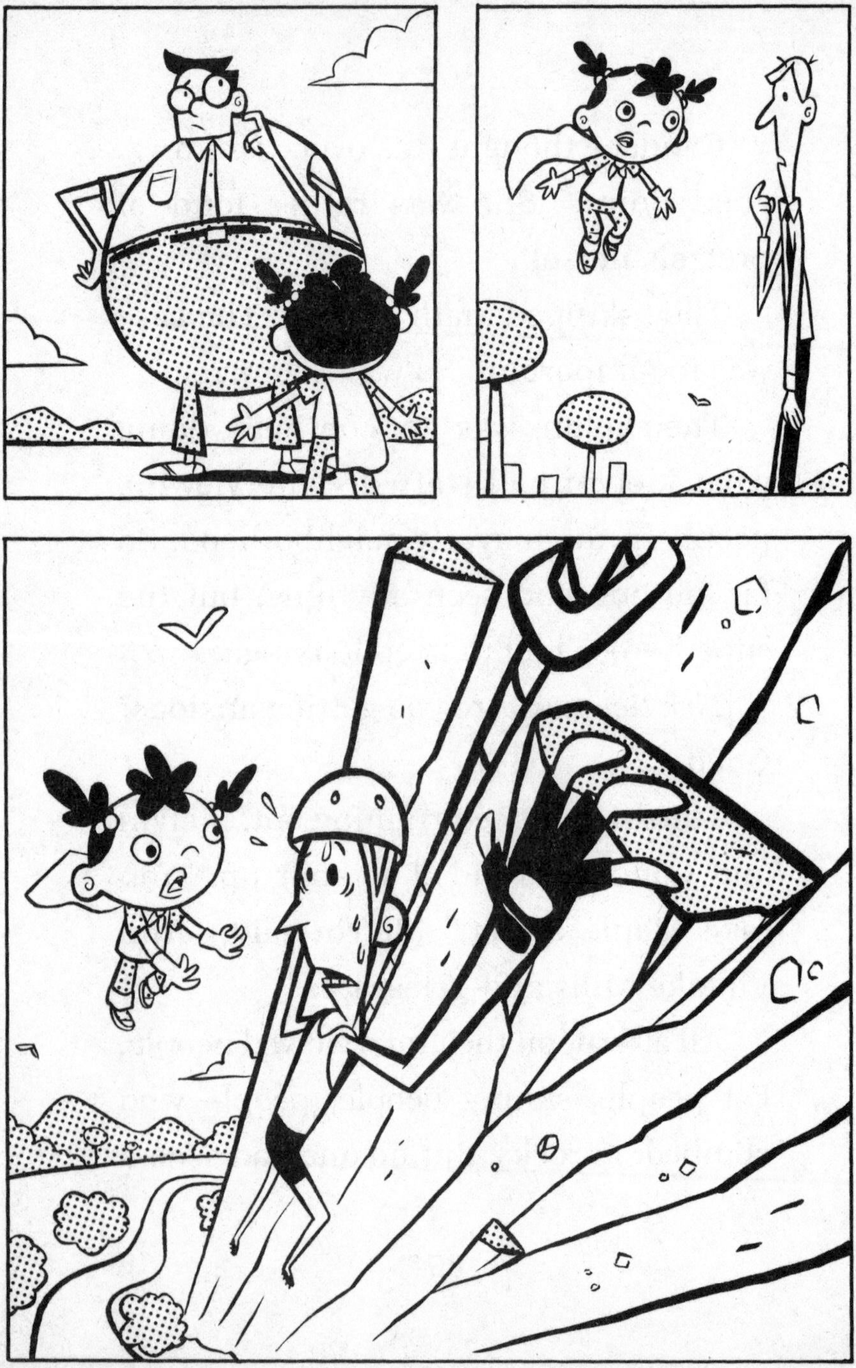

thing. The kidnappers were good, all right. They were pros.

Melvin and Candace met up again at the end of the day.

"Any leads?" Melvin asked.

"None. You?"

"Nope." Melvin walked Candace home. He didn't feel like flying. He didn't feel like crashing, splatting, thudding, and kabonking after such a long day of failing. "We might have to work all night on this one, Candace."

"Anything to keep me away from homework would be much appreciated."

Late that night Melvin came back to Candace's house and threw a pebble at her bedroom window. This was part of the Sneaking Out at Night Code. Someone had to throw a pebble at a bedroom window. It was a rule.

Candace opened her window and looked down at her partner in uncrime. "I wish you'd come earlier. I ended up doing *homework. Eew!*"

Eew, indeed!

Candace joined Melvin and they took off. Or at least Candace did. Melvin joined her on the fifth try, as usual.

"I have an idea," Candace said as they hovered above the trees.

"I'm listening."

"We interviewed every person in the mayor's neighborhood and no one saw a thing, right?"

"Right."

"What about animals?"

Melvin scratched his head. It was his

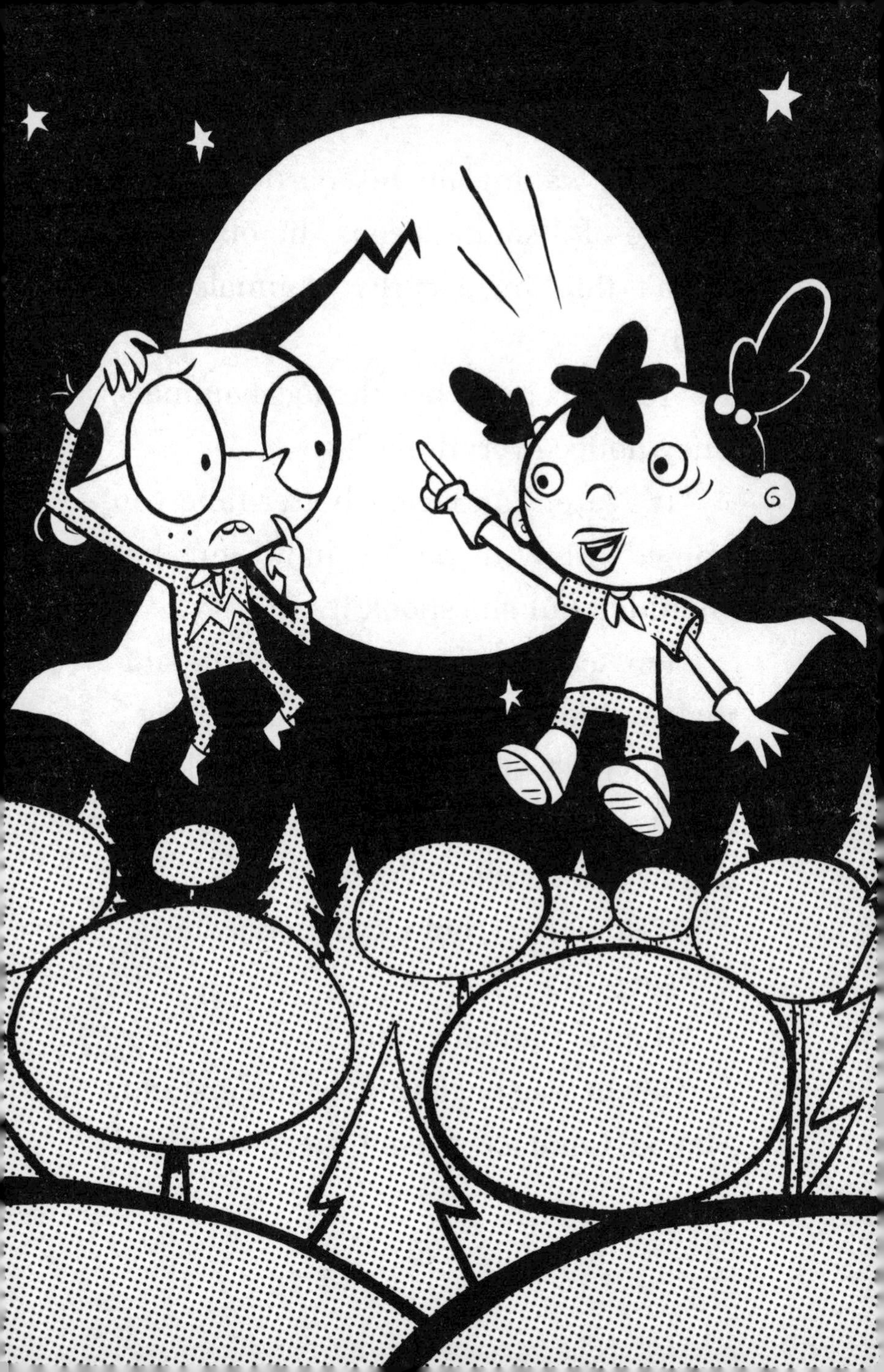

fault for waking up his partner in the middle of a sound sleep. She obviously wasn't thinking clearly. "Animals?" he said.

"Yes, let's interview the local animals. They notice everything."

"It's late, Candace. I better take you home." Melvin put a hand on her shoulder, but she shook it off.

"I'm serious. If we interview the animals we may come up with something."

Melvin gave her a look. "I don't know about you, but I'm not exactly fluent in dog or cat, let alone lizard."

"Neither am I, but I know a rat who is."

"Hugo?"

"Hugo," Candace said.

Melvin was beginning to understand. Maybe Candace wasn't sleep-deprived after all. But there was a problem. After Hugo conducted the interviews, how would they get the information from him? Melvin couldn't speak rat.

"Your plan might not work," he told her as they flew over to his tree house.

"What do you mean?"

"I can't speak rat."

Candace grinned. "That's okay. I can."

THE BIRTH OF A SIDEKICK

The mayor, who was also the mad scientist, was pretty upset that someone had stolen Schnitzel. He loved that little guy, even though Schnitzel had stolen the milk shake . . . uh . . . evil potion. Ever since then, the mad scientist had been trying to whip up another one, so that he could make his son, Mike, more evil. He had to do something. Mike had recently invited a superhero right into his lair . . . uh . . . home.

Mike, of course, didn't want any of this mad scientist business. His goal in life was to be a superhero's sidekick. He subscribed to *Sidekick's Monthly*, where they advertised for sidekicks. He had also ordered a sidekick's uniform and was in his room trying it on when his mad scientist/mayor father burst in.

"What's going on here?" his father demanded.

"Uh . . . I'm trying on my . . . uh . . . my costume . . . for Halloween. Yeah, that's it. My Halloween costume. How do you like this purple cape, Dad? "

The mad scientist raised one of his hairy eyebrows. "Halloween is months away."

"You can never be too prepared. You taught me that, Dad. Always be prepared."

"Be prepared when you're trying to take over the world!" He looked closely at his son's sidekick uniform.

"What's with the tights? Are you supposed be some kind of elf?"

The son snorted. "Elves don't wear capes, Dad."

The mad scientist went out of the room, slamming the door behind him. It was bad enough that someone had stolen his dog. Now he had a son in tights!

After his father left the room, Mike went back to reading *Sidekick's Monthly*. There were lots of interesting articles— "Keeping the Sidekick's Code," "Cape Design and Maintenance," and "Superheroes Are from Mars, Sidekicks Are from Venus."

One thing was clear from the reading he'd done. In order to get a job as a sidekick, you had to prove yourself first. Mike decided to do just that. He would prove himself to the superhero world *and* to his father. He would find Schnitzel and bring him back.

He adjusted his cape, gave his tights a tug, and set off.

While the mad scientist's son was out looking to solve the case of the missing wiener dog, Melvin and Candace were trying to explain their plan to Hugo.

"Squeak squeakity," Hugo replied.

"What did he say?" Melvin asked Candace.

"He said he'll do anything to save a dog. Just don't ask him to save a *cat*."

Melvin picked up Hugo and placed him on his shoulder. "Hold on tight," he told him. "Up, up, and—"

"Wait a second!" Candace grabbed Hugo. "Better let me carry him."

"Why?"

"Crash, splat, thud, kabonk? You don't want to squash our Dr. Doolittle here."

"Good point." Melvin climbed down from the tree house. "Up, up, and away." And, of course, it was just as Candace predicted. He crashed, he splatted, he thudded, he kabonked. On the fifth try he was up and flying, with his partner in uncrime and his faithful pet Hugo alongside him.

"Squeak," Hugo said.

"What did he say?" Melvin asked.

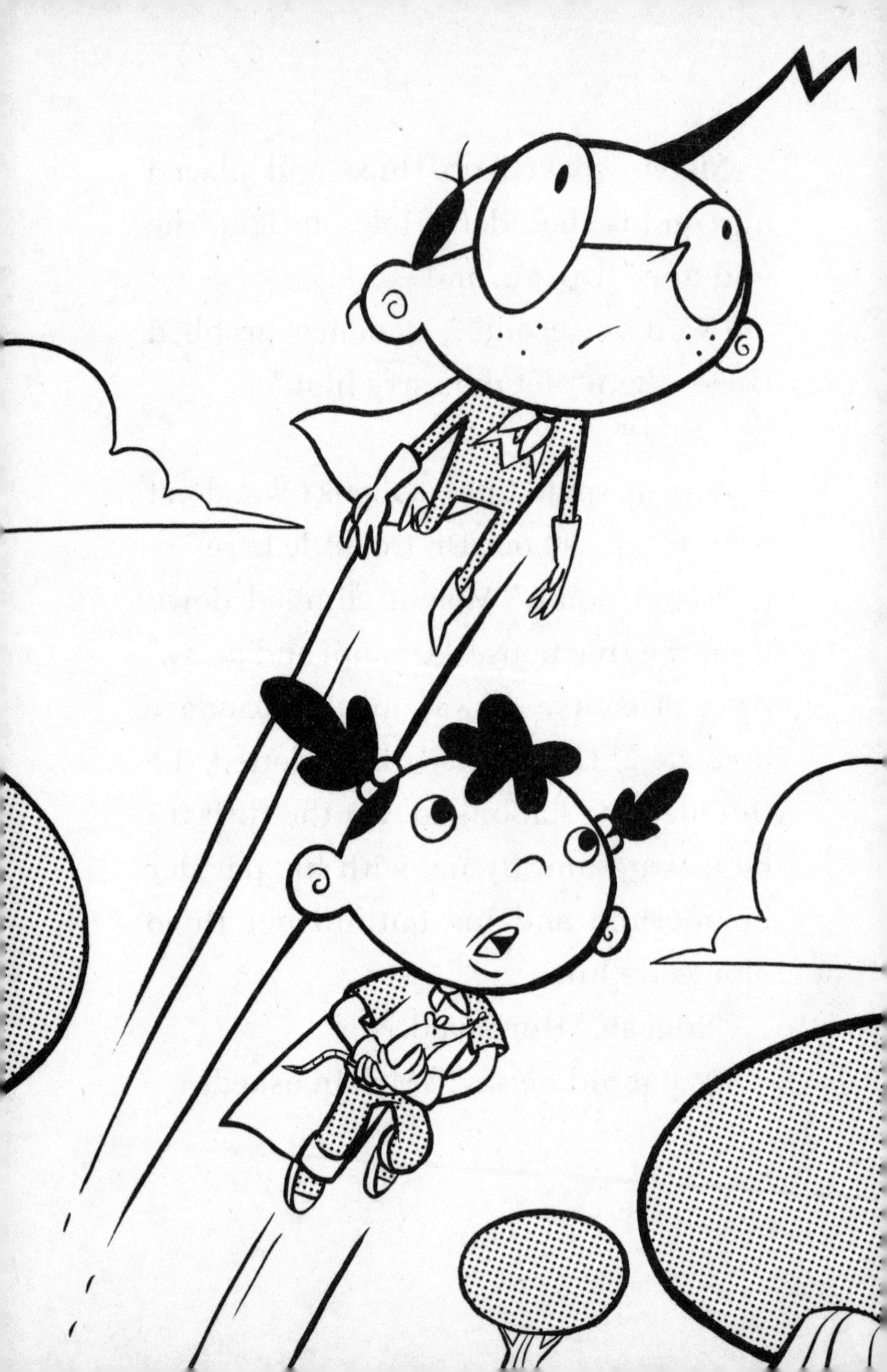

"He's just glad that I'm the one who's carrying him."

They sped across the sky. Somewhere there was an animal who had seen something the night Schnitzel was kidnapped. They had to find him before time ran out.

Tick tick tick.

"I sure wish the narrator would stop doing that," Candace said.

Melvin nodded. "I know what you mean."

JETHRO GULL

"I miss our lair at Macy's," Brittany said.

"Me, too, but there's nothing we can do about that now," Chantelle replied. This was true. Macy's had been a good lair. You had to love a lair where you could try on the latest fashions while coming up with devious and sinister plans. "For our next crime we'll, like, move back to the mall. How does that sound?"

"Awesome."

For now, the two Valley girls–turned-dognappers had to use Chantelle's bedroom for their lair. While they waited for the mayor to turn over control of the city to them, they discussed the future and the changes they'd make.

"How about Shopping Day?" Brittany suggested. "All high school kids get a day off to go shopping."

"Totally!" Chantelle said. "And no homework—*ever!*"

Two airheads putting their heads together was a dangerous thing. Los Angeles would never be the same.

Fortunately, Melvin, Candace, and Hugo were on the job. They spotted two stray dogs sniffing a fire hydrant and dropped from the sky to ask a few questions.

"Squeak squeak?" Hugo said, giving his whiskers a little twitch.

One of the dogs looked up. "*Grrrr.*"

Candace asked Hugo to interpret.

"Squeaker squeakity," Hugo replied.

"What did he say?" Melvin asked.

"According to Hugo the dog said, '*Grrrr.*'"

"Tell him to try again."

Hugo tried again, this time with a little more whisker twitching. You can never have too much whisker twitching.

This time the dogs barked and ruffed.

"They haven't seen anything," Candace said after Hugo passed along the message.

And so the threesome moved on. They interviewed a few squirrels, a cat, and a seagull named Jethro. But just like the dogs, they hadn't seen a thing on the night of the dognapping.

"What do we do now?" Candace asked as Jethro took to the sky.

"Keep an eye on Jethro," Melvin said. "You know what seagulls do once they're airborne."

"I was talking about the case."

Melvin pointed to two hawks sitting on a tree limb. "More interviews," he said.

Candace picked up Hugo and lifted off the ground. Melvin did things his way.

The two hawks eyed Melvin and Candace with suspicion. They looked at Hugo and drooled.

One of the hawks squawked at the other. "Is that a wiener dog or a rat?"

"I think it's a rat, but don't quote me."

All Melvin and Candace heard was hawk language, of course. But Hugo knew what they were saying. He also saw their sharp claws and their drool. Lucky for him, he had two superheroes to protect him.

He looked at one of the hawks. "Squeaker squeakity?"

At last, somebody who knew something. The hawks had seen two girls in the neighborhood, one of them holding a gagged wiener dog or rat.

Hugo asked for a description of the girls and their car. Then he translated the information to Candace, who relayed it to Melvin, who jotted it down in a notepad. This was good detective work—complicated, but good.

Now they had something to go on. Now they could solve the case.

VALLEY GIRLS

Word got around that two superheroes and a rat were hot on the trail. And these two superheroes were none other than Melvin Beederman and Candace Brinkwater.

"Like, what do we do now?" Brittany asked. She knew full well that bad guys trembled at the sound of Melvin's name. They probably did the same at the sound of Candace's.

There was only one thing to do—make bologna sandwiches. The two superheroes grew weak in the presence of bologna. But would it be enough?

"There's something else we can do," Chantelle said, finishing the last sandwich. "Follow me."

They went down to the garage, where their Valley girl/dognapper vehicle was parked. Chantelle turned to Brittany. "Melvin is as fast as a speeding bullet, right?"

"That's what they say."

"Have you ever heard of Gamma Drive?"

"Nope. What is it?"

Chantelle popped the hood of the car and lifted it up. "If it's, like, good enough for evil aliens, it's good enough for us."

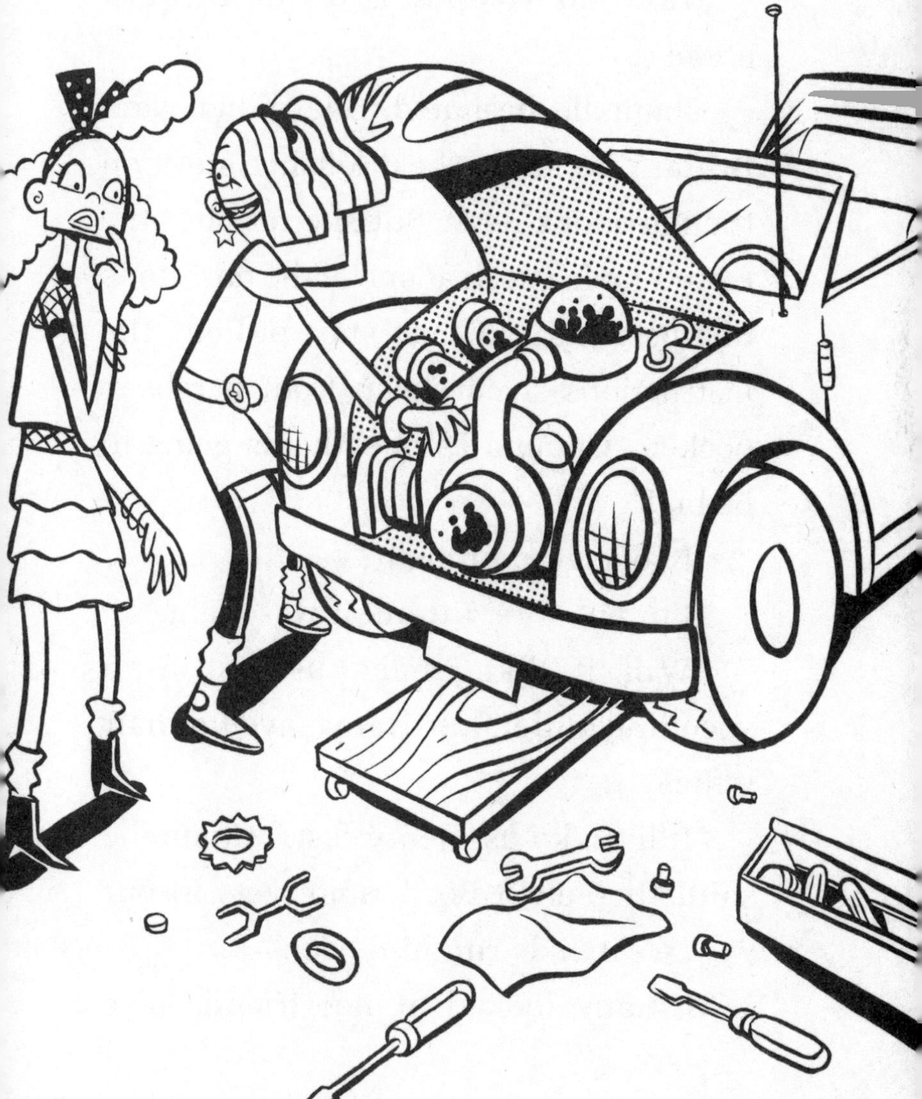

"How do you know about the evil aliens?"

Chantelle hesitated. She didn't want Brittany to know she'd left her story on the narrator's desk. But she told her the rest. "I took a peek at one of the narrator's manuscripts." Then she pulled the instructions she'd stolen from her back pocket. "Gamma Drive—this is going to be big!"

"Book seven or eight?"

"I'm not sure. I think it was eight."

"Will it, like, make us fast as a speeding bullet?" Brittany gave her hair a flick.

"It'll make us plenty fast," Chantelle said. "If Melvin Beederman gets in our way, we'll, like, run him over."

Brittany looked at her friend. "I've

never run over a superhero before, but
I'm very open to new experiences."

"So am I," Chantelle said, grabbing
a wrench. "Let's get
to work."

They did. They worked and worked and worked. "Are you sure you're reading that right?" Brittany asked after some time. "Duct tape and a screwdriver?"

Chantelle nodded and pointed to the instructions. "Unless the narrator got it wrong."

The narrator never gets things wrong!

In the end, the car not only had the superfast Gamma Drive, but it was extremely quiet, which would be good for sneaking up behind superheroes and running them over.

This gave Chantelle an idea. She closed the hood of the car and looked at Brittany. "Why wait for them to find us?"

"Who?"

"Melvin Beederman and his sidekick.

We have, like, Gamma Drive now. Let's hunt them down and run them over. Then nothing can stop us from taking over the city."

Brittany agreed that this was a good idea. She was really looking forward to being queen of her very own city. And so they grabbed the bologna sandwiches and set off, silently, into the night. With any luck, Melvin would soon go *SPLAT* like he'd never gone *SPLAT* before. So would Candace.

The car zoomed, maybe not as fast as a speeding bullet, but pretty close. Close enough to hunt down a superhero or two—especially if they didn't hear anything coming.

"Too bad we don't have a cloaking

device," Brittany said. "That would, like, make it easier to sneak up on them."

"Shoot!" Chantelle said. "I should have read more of that manuscript. Aliens have such cool stuff."

SPEAKING OF ALIENS ...

While Brittany and Chantelle were out looking for a couple of superheroes to run down, the evil aliens finally reached Alphacentory. The question is Did they turn the right way or the wrong way? The right way would take them toward Earth. The wrong way would take them someplace else.

The narrator is not telling. This is how he keeps readers in suspense. It's kind of like that *tick tick tick* thing, only it involves creatures from outer space.

If it's really upsetting that you don't know whether they are heading for Earth or not, please log on to narrator-complaints@peevedreader.wah.

But back to our story. Melvin, Candace, and Hugo now had a description of the dognappers and their vehicle. It would not be long before they tracked them down and captured them, after saying such things as "Not so fast!"

"What if we get there too late?" Candace asked.

"We still have a few hours," Melvin told her. "These two are pros. They won't do anything to Schnitzel until the time is up."

This was what Melvin hoped anyway. You never knew when you were dealing with bad guys . . . uh . . . bad girls. A few hours wasn't long, especially when you were dealing with bad girls.

"What do you know? It's finally happened," Candace said.

"What has?" Melvin asked.

"Now the narrator is repeating him-*self*!"

"It's late in the story. It happens."

The two superheroes flew over the city, Hugo still perched on Candace's shoulder. The narrator didn't even have to say *tick tick tick*. They felt it. Time was running out.

It was not only late in the story—it was just plain late. Melvin was usually sound asleep at this hour (unless Hugo was snoring). So was Candace.

They searched and searched, growing more tired by the minute. They could hardly keep their eyes open. Finally, they decided to land and search on foot. Flying when you were sleepy was an accident waiting to happen. Better to be on solid ground.

"What did the hawk say the car looked like again?" Melvin was trying to stay awake, and talking seemed to be the best way.

"Powder-blue convertible," Candace said with a yawn.

They were on the outskirts of Los

Angeles now, having already searched downtown. There were cranes and bulldozers and dump trucks, stacks of lumber, and half-built houses.

"Holy construction site!" Melvin said. "This would be a great place for a bad-guy lair."

Holy construction site, indeed! It *would* be. The only thing better, of course, would be an abandoned warehouse. But these are Valley girls we're talking about. They live to shop. They might ruin their new jeans in a construction site lair.

Melvin, Candace, and Hugo moved cautiously. Dark shadows loomed all around. It would be a great place for sinister and devious people to hide out. But the shadows were empty, unbeknownst to Melvin and team.

The real danger was in the car behind them, the one driven by a teenage girl, the one silently racing toward them at Gamma Speed.

AHHHH-HEE-AHHHH!

"Step on it, Brittany!" Chantelle stared out the window. She was so nervous that she'd been eating the bologna sandwiches without thinking. Now they were gone. At least they had the car. It zoomed silently forward. Maybe it wasn't quite as fast as a speeding bullet, but it was pretty darn fast.

"I have, like, the pedal to the metal already." Brittany pointed to the Gamma dial, where the needle was on red. She

121

didn't bother flicking her hair. The wind did it for her.

Up ahead, two superheroes and a rat turned. There was no time to move, no time react at all. And that's when they heard it—

A cry ripped through the night. *"Ahhhh-hee-ahhhh!"*

Was it Tarzan? Was it the Lone Ranger with his faithful companion Tonto? Was it some guy who just felt like yelling?

It was none of those.

The Gamma Drive–enhanced convertible driven by the evil-potion–enhanced girl was a few feet away—maybe inches—when a streak of purple flashed in front of her! Swinging on a cable suspended from a crane, Mike, aspiring sidekick, snatched Melvin, Candace, and Hugo out from in front of the speeding car.

Just in time. Just in the nick of time, to be exact!

But the bad girls were not giving up.

"Turn this thing around and try again," Chantelle yelled.

"I'm on it," Brittany yelled back. She slammed on the brakes and whipped the steering wheel to one side. The car spun, and she hit the gas, once more speeding toward not two superheroes, but . . . *three*?

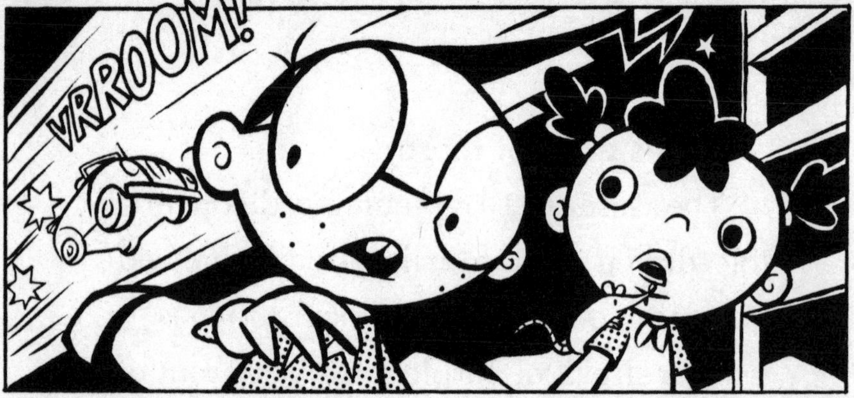
VRROOM!

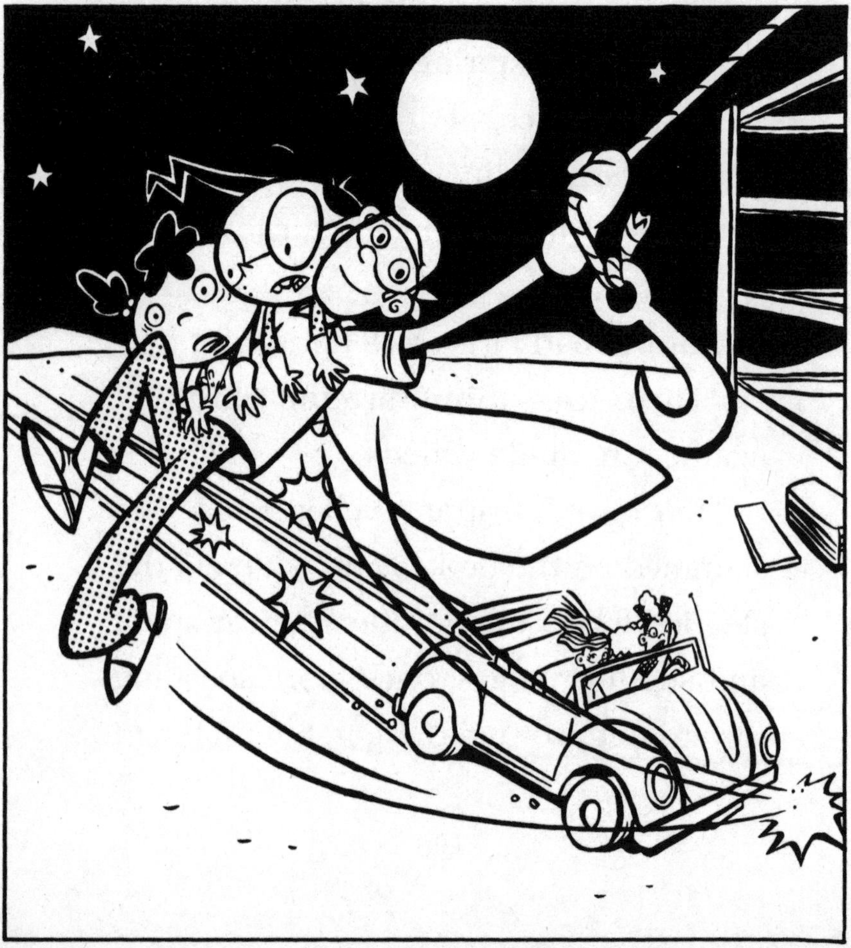

This time they were ready for her. Or were they? A car with Gamma Drive was as powerful as a speeding locomotive, and stopping trains wasn't Melvin's best skill.

The car raced toward them.

"Better leave this one to us," Melvin told the guy in the purple cape. He had not yet recognized the mad scientist's son with whom he'd had tea. He was just some guy in a cape who might or might not be a real superhero.

"I'm here to help," Mike said.

At the last minute Melvin pushed him out of the way. Then he and Candace grabbed the front of the car as it struck. They dug their feet into the ground. But the car did not slow. Melvin and Candace put everything they had into it. Meanwhile, Hugo jumped onto Mike's shoulder to watch.

Two crazed teenagers in the car. Two superheroes digging in as the car raced. It pushed them the entire length of the construction site, crashed into a bull-dozer—and the engine died.

"We did it!" Brittany said.

"The city is, like, ours!"

Mike and Hugo stared in disbelief. Melvin and Candace were gone. They'd defeated the McNastys, they'd bested Joe the Bad Guy, not to mention the Spaz Brothers, and here they were, done in by a couple of girls from the Valley.

"Squeak?" said Hugo. This may have meant "Say it isn't so." Or it might have been "I miss Melvin Beederman."

Candace would know what he was saying. Only she was no longer around to interpret.

All was silent in the construction site as the dust settled. Even the evil Valley girls were quiet.

And then . . .

There was a tremendous sound of steel bending. The car, still occupied by the crazed teenagers, lifted off the ground, and there stood Melvin and Candace beneath it, holding it up. They turned the car over and dumped Brittany and Chantelle onto the ground.

"Curses!" Chantelle said.

"Yeah, curses!" Brittany repeated. This was what villains said when someone foiled their evil plans.

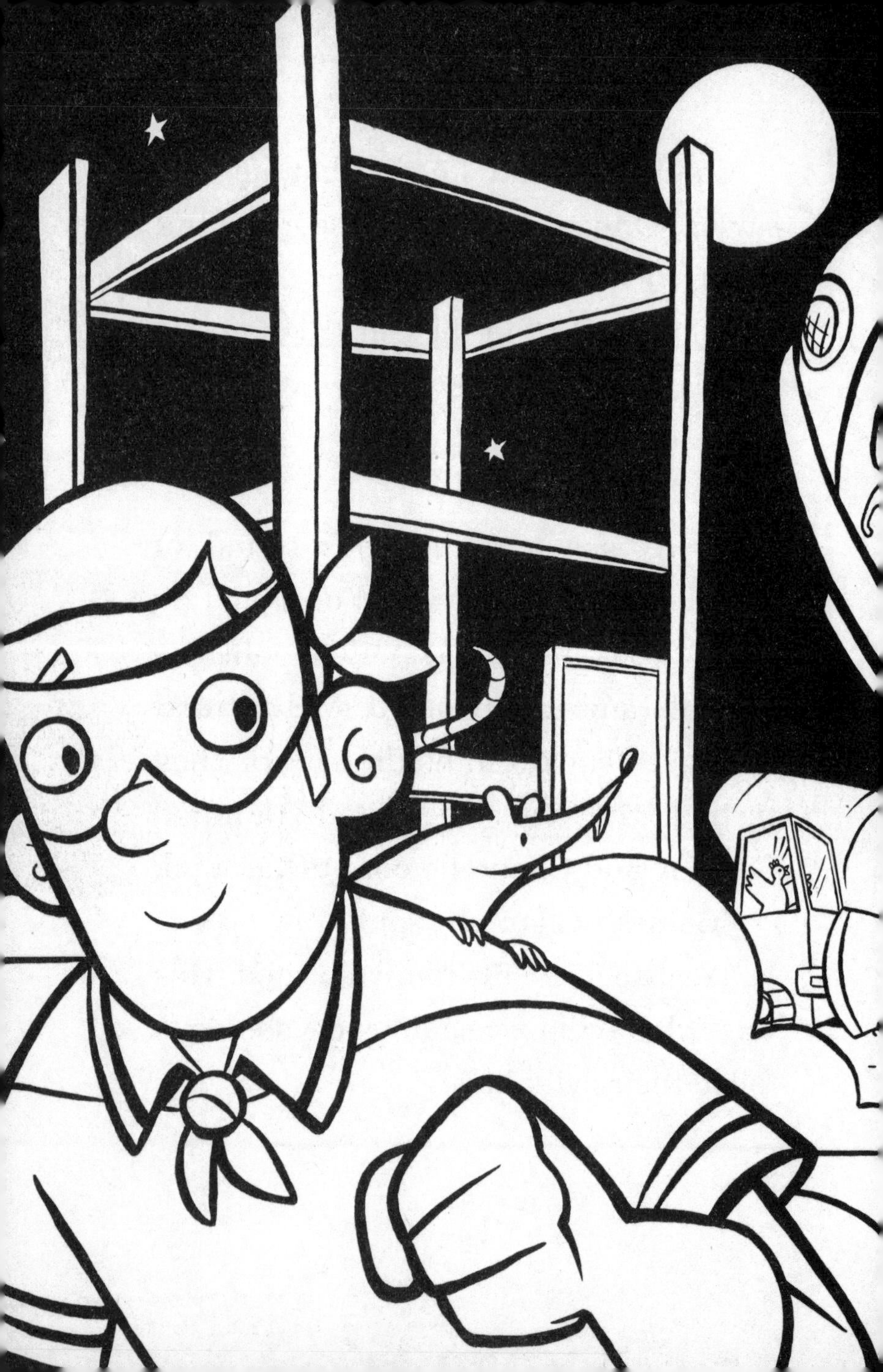

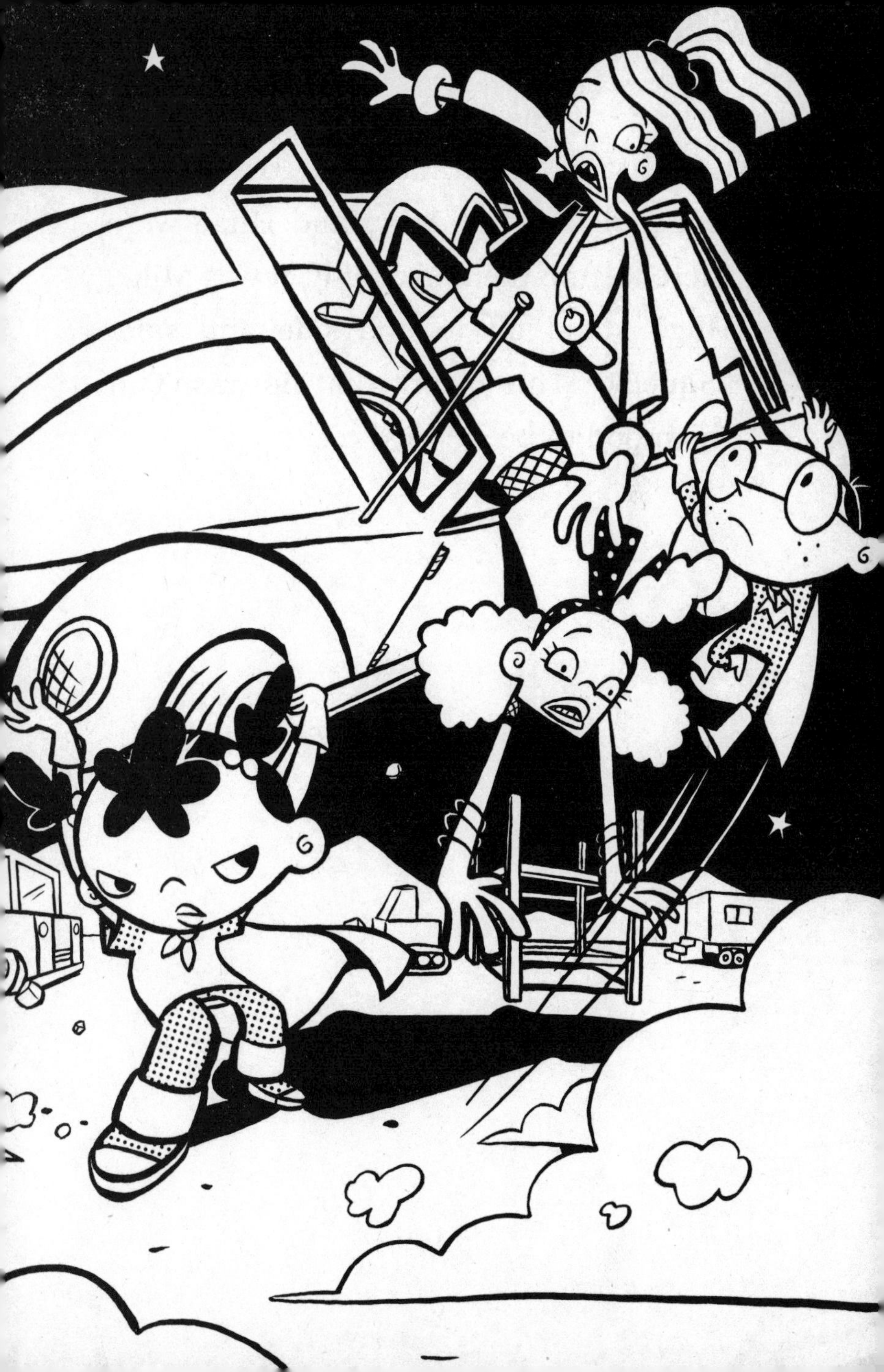

Brittany and Chantelle got to their feet and ran. But Mike and Hugo were there to stop them. Actually, it was Mike. Hugo stood off to one side and said, "Squeak." This meant that he wasn't in the mood to be stepped on.

A STRANGE TURN OF EVENTS

Schnitzel was returned to the mayor/mad scientist, who, in a strange turn of events, didn't press charges against Brittany and Chantelle. Instead, he adopted them. He was impressed with their Gamma Drive invention, but mostly with their overall evilness. Unlike his purple-cape-wearing son, these two girls had real potential as future mad scientists.

The mayor decided to quit his job

with the city of Los Angeles and devote himself full time to mad scientist work. With his new evil daughters and a certain amount of luck, he'd be taking over the world in no time.

Schnitzel, of course, could not believe his little dog ears. And ears never lie! How could he live with the very people who had kidnapped and gagged him? When Chantelle and Brittany moved in, Schnitzel moved out. He would go someplace where they really needed him—the local Alley Rat community. He would lead them in their revolt against the Alley Cats.

And so he set off, keeping an eye out for birds of prey and singing, "I'm a wiener dog, not a rat." Maybe he wasn't a rat *now*. But he soon would be.

The mad scientist's son, Mike, also decided not to stick around. He had proven himself as a sidekick by saving Melvin and Candace, and he knew that somewhere there was a superhero who needed help saving the world.

He met up with Melvin and Candace at the local pretzel and root beer parlor, which was right next to Bert's Bar and Grill.

"Thanks for coming to our rescue," Melvin said to Mike. "We didn't hear that car coming."

"That's Gamma Drive for you," Candace added.

"You're welcome," Mike said with a smile. It was nice to hang out with a pair of real superheroes. He knew he was one step away from landing a sidekick job.

And with Melvin's and Candace's help, he was sure he would.

"We could write you a letter of recommendation," Melvin suggested.

"That would be great," Mike said.

After a few snacks and three large root beer floats, the three of them left the parlor and walked slowly down the street. They were tired from their adventures, but happy. Once again, they'd foiled an evil plot. Even though the Valley girls weren't in jail, the superheroes had stopped them from their devious and sinister deeds, and that was all that mattered.

The street was deserted, but they were not alone. High above them a seagull named Jethro circled. He knew a target when he saw one. Suddenly he dove at the three people in capes below him, letting out a triumphant "Caw."

Something went *SPLAT*.

And for the first time in a long while, it wasn't Melvin Beederman.

WHO IS THE NARRATOR?

The narrator came from a long line of narrators. His dad was a narrator. His mom was a narrator. Even his goldfish was a narrator—you may have read the literary classic *Goldifish and the Three Bears*. But the narrator didn't want to follow in the footsteps of his parents, not to mention his fish. He decided he'd rather see the world. And see the world he did. When he wasn't climbing mountains in Nepal or running with the bulls in Spain, he could be found wrestling polar bears in the Arctic, swimming with sharks off the coast of California, or dancing the night away at Fast Eddy's Amazing Disco and All-Night Car Wash.

For a future narrator he sure could cut a rug.

But something happened one night that would change his life forever. He was confronted in a dark alley by three thugs and a bad guy named Fred. Did the narrator use his famous polar bear wrestling skills? Did he run like a Spanish bull? Did he cut a rug right there on the street?

Nope. He simply talked his way out of it. After all, the gift of gab ran in his family. Those thugs' ears were dazzled!

The narrator has been telling stories ever since, especially about an adventuring superhero named Melvin Beederman, his sidekick Candace Brinkwater . . . and a few guys named Fred.

Alley Rats Defeat Alley Cats, 5-4

AP — LOS ANGELES.

Led by the largest rat seen in these parts in many years, the local rat community rose up last night to defeat the local cats who have been in control of the city's alleys and open fields for centuries. "The rats are a force to be reckoned with," said the new leader. Actually, what he said was "Bark bark bark bark," but what he meant was "The rats are a force to be reckoned with."